THE
FORESHADOWING

Also by Marcus Sedgwick

The Book of Dead Days
The Dark Flight Down
The Dark Horse
Floodland
Witch Hill

THE
FORESHADOWING

Marcus Sedgwick

Orion
Children's Books

First published in Great Britain in 2005
by Orion Children's Books
a division of the Orion Publishing Group Ltd
Orion House
5 Upper St Martin's Lane
London WC2H 9EA

A catalogue record for this book is available
from the British Library

ISBN 1 84255 219 8

Typeset at The Spartan Press Ltd,
Lymington, Hants

Printed in Great Britain by
Clays Ltd, St Ives plc

www.orionbooks.co.uk

For Fiona Kennedy
my superb editor

Acknowledgments

I would like to thank the following for their assistance with the research for this book. Helen Pugh and the staff of the Red Cross Museum and Archives Department; the helpful members of staff at the Imperial War Museum; Martin Nimmo and Sue Rubenstein of mybrightonandhove.com; and Elizabeth Garrett, for her research into Clifton Terrace, and Brighton in general, in 1916.

I have found many books invaluable for capturing the spirit of the time including Vera Brittain's *Testament of Youth* and *Chronicle of Youth*, Enid Bagnold's *A Diary Without Dates*, Robert Graves' *Goodbye to All That*, and Captain Dunn's *The War the Infantry Knew*. *A Brief Jolly Change*, the diaries of Henry Peerless, edited by Edward Fenton, was not only informative, but delightful to me, since it features members of my own family.

So, believe me, or not,
What does it matter now?
Fate works its way,
And soon you will stand and say,
my words were true.

From *Agamemnon* by Aeschylus

Part One

101

I was five when I first saw the future. Now I am seventeen.

I can't remember much about it. Or maybe I should say I *couldn't* remember much about it, until now.

For years all I could recall was laughter, nervous laughter, and later, silence, then later still, anger. I felt ashamed, guilty, hurt when I thought about it, but I had quite forgotten what *it* was. Or rather, I had made myself forget.

Memories, half-hidden for twelve years, have started to surface, in bits and pieces, until I see a picture of that day long ago, when I was just a little girl.

We weren't living in Clifton Terrace then, with my wonderful view of the sea, but I don't know where we did live. There was a big garden, bigger than the one we have here. I was playing in this garden with another girl, about my own age. Edgar and Tom were young then too, and even played with us sometimes when they weren't trying to fall out of the big cooking apple tree.

It was summer, and the girl and I were best friends. Her name was Clare and she was the daughter of friends of my parents. It was a long and happy afternoon, but eventually it was time for Clare to go home.

And this is the part I had pushed away and hidden in the depths of my memory for so many years.

I was standing in the hall, giggling with Clare while grown-up chat buzzed above our heads.

Then I said something. I said something that stopped the grown-ups talking and started the silence.

'Why does Clare have to die?' I asked.

Because no one said anything, I thought they hadn't heard me, so I tried again.

'I don't want Clare to die tomorrow.'

Then they did start talking, and I knew they had heard, because Mother was scolding me, and Clare started crying and her mother took her away.

I was wrong. Clare didn't die next day. But I was only five, and, I suppose, didn't understand that tomorrow meant something more specific than *soon*.

Soon, however, I *was* right. Clare died of tuberculosis. It came quickly and there was nothing the doctors could do to save her. I can remember very clearly now wishing I could have helped her. Stopped her dying.

Then the silence started.

Not long after, we moved house, here to Clifton Terrace, and gradually I forgot all about that day when I was five.

Until now.

I have seen the future again, and it is death. I can no longer pretend it is my imagination.

I wasn't sure. That I had dreamed about something that came to be might just have been a coincidence. It was a month ago that I dreamt George had been killed. The morning after my dream Father was reading *The Times* at breakfast.

'George Yates,' he said, without looking up. 'That's Edgar's friend, isn't it?'

Mother nodded.

Father read from the paper, still without looking up.

' "Captain George Yates died of wounds, Vermelles, 26 September, 1915." '

I was too shocked to know what to think.

'Poor George,' said Tom.

'Poor Edgar,' Mother said, thinking of her other son. Her elder son, away somewhere in France.

Clumsily she began stacking the plates from breakfast. Tom, my other brother, rose to help her.

'Edgar is fine,' Father said. 'He's a strong young man.'

Now he looked up from his paper for the first time, to fix his eyes on Tom.

'And where's that blasted girl?' he went on, meaning Molly, our maid. 'Don't we pay *her* enough to do that?'

Tom ignored him and carried the plates out to the kitchen.

'No harm will come to the strong,' Father said. 'The brave.'

He started to read the casualty lists again. I don't know why he has to do it. He spends all day with the sick and the dying in the hospital.

'Where is Molly?' Father snapped.

'Cook's away and Molly's busy,' said Mother.

'Alexandra,' Father sighed. 'Help your brother.'

I jumped up and tried to lend a hand, but I could only think about George. He had been at the front; he had been killed. That was not unusual, not anymore. But I had dreamt that it had happened, the night *before* news of it had reached us.

Was that possible?

Over the following days I tried not to dwell on it.

I continued my studies during the day with Miss Garrett and in the evenings I sat with Mother. She's always busy organising her circle of friends, as well as running the house, and Cook, and Molly, who's sweet, but scatterbrained.

I tried again to persuade Father to let me help around the wards, but still he refused. He says it's not fitting for a girl like me, and once his mind is made up, it usually stays that way.

Although I tried to forget George, I couldn't. Images of his death came to me; I don't know where from. One morning I was sitting at my mirror, brushing my hair and thinking how long it was getting, when into my head came a picture of George's mother reading the telegram that gave her the news.

I saw George caught on the wire that we're always hearing about, but that may have been my imagination. I don't know how he died.

I was frightened, but the days passed and I told myself it was a coincidence. Thousands of men are being killed in France each week, and the fact that I dreamt about the death of one of them could be nothing more than chance. I even wondered whether I might have already heard about George's death and not taken it in. Maybe it had already been posted in the lists and Father had missed it. It seemed unlikely, but I clung to this explanation until time allowed me to put it to one corner of my mind, if not to forget about it entirely.

But after what happened yesterday, I can no longer pretend it is my imagination.

Mother and I were walking down Middle Street. We passed the Hippodrome, where I used to love to go to see the circus when I was little. I dawdled outside, remembering a silly act we'd seen there once featuring Dinky, the high-diving dog. Mother pulled my hand.

'Come on, Sasha,' she said. Sometimes she still uses my pet name, as though I'm her little Russian princess.

The sea was in front of us. It's late October and there was a grim grey sky above us. Waves were being whipped against the sea wall by fierce winds. As so often the town was full of soldiers; a mass of khaki uniforms.

We would have walked up to the hospital to see Father, but it looked as if it might start to rain any moment. People scurried past us, a horse and empty cart hurried for home, its driver glancing nervously at the sky.

'We'll take the tram,' Mother said, so we turned and cut

through to the Old Steine, to the stop outside Marlborough House.

There was a long queue. Everything was perfectly ordinary as we waited for the tram. When it arrived the ladies jostled a little to be first on, but in a good-tempered way.

Mother looked at the gathering clouds.

'Come on,' she said, taking my hand.

'No,' I said.

She glanced round at me, surprised.

'Don't play games, Alexandra, I'm cold and it's about to rain.'

'I'm not,' I said.

I didn't know what was wrong.

I just knew I didn't want to be on the tram. That I *mustn't* be on it.

A soldier waiting behind us was impatient.

'Come on, darling,' he said. 'Get a move on.'

But I didn't move.

I could see Mother was embarrassed. The soldier pushed past, bumping into me, as he got on to the tram. He spun round on the step. I stared straight into his eyes.

'Sorry, gorgeous, can't hang about,' he said. There was a cheeky smile on his lips, but as he looked at me, the smile lost its life, and died on his face.

I *knew* he was going to die. I don't know what else I can say. I saw it. Not in France, not in the war, but soon. Here.

'Are you feeling all right?' Mother said, not cross now, thinking I was unwell.

'I don't want to go on the tram.'

'Sasha . . .' Mother began, and then stopped. She sighed.

People pushed on to the tram, but the soldier stood on the

step, still looking at me. Mother saw him and I think it was that, and no other reason, that made her let me have my way. I knew what she thought about 'rough' men.

'We'll walk,' she said, and the tram moved off.

As it went, the soldier was still staring at me.

I watched it go. Mother tugged at my arm, impatiently, but I couldn't move. It was as though I was rooted to the spot. It all happened very slowly then. But somehow very quickly, too. The tram got up to speed and rumbled away towards Grand Parade.

The rain began to lash down then, very suddenly.

A wheel lifted from the tracks somehow; on a point maybe. The tram came off the rails, and laid down on one side, with a tremendous crash. It hit a wall and there was a shower of sparks and rubble.

I was aware of noise all around us. The noise of the tram hitting the wall seemed to take the longest time to reach us, and to be the quietest sound. The sound of screaming was the loudest.

Mother finally dragged me away. Last night, before I went to bed, I asked her why we had left, and she told me that there was nothing we could have done. That lots of people, too many perhaps, had immediately swarmed around the tram, to help others off. The police had arrived, and ambulance cars took the injured to the Royal Sussex, where Father used to work until he was put in charge of the Dyke Road Hospital. I still feel I should have done something. I should have helped.

This morning I read in the paper that most people in the accident had not been too badly hurt, but that one man had been killed.

A soldier.

Thinking back to yesterday, I remember feeling one emotion from my mother. Fear. But not fear of the accident.

Although she doesn't know that I have remembered, I know what she's thinking about. She's thinking about a day long ago, when I was five.

War. That's all there seems to be.

It's all around us. Nothing is unaffected by it, no one is immune. Everyone has suffered, everyone has lost someone, or at least knows someone who has. There seems to be little else in the newspapers, little that anyone talks about.

It is over a year now since the war began, but it seems no time at all since I sat listening to my brothers arguing about it, and with Father too. I was sixteen then, and not supposed to have an opinion. But I sat and listened, in the corner of the room, while they talked. I can't recall precisely, but it may have been the actual day we declared war on Germany.

Edgar and Father were very excited, Tom was quiet.

'You don't want to enlist in the ranks,' Father said to Edgar. 'You can take a commission. With your OTC experience you'll be snapped up.'

'It would have been better if I was a regular already,' Edgar said. 'It'll all be over before I get there. By the time I get a commission and hang around on a parade ground for months, it'll all be over.'

'Then better you don't delay. Move quickly and you'll get your share of the glory.'

I was listening to Father, but I was watching Tom. Edgar and

Father stood by the dining room table, poring over the morning's *Times*.

Tom was gazing out at the sea lapping way beyond the West Pier, his thin frame silhouetted by a bright summer's sun outside. It made me think as I often did that it was hard to imagine my two brothers were related. Edgar's so much bigger, and stronger. He never seems to worry about things, he just does them, whereas Tom worries about everything and everyone. I'm told that once, when I was little, I was crying about a dead bird in the garden, and he put his arm round me and told me that animals go to heaven too. I don't suppose that's true, but he wanted to make me happy. That's how much he worries about people.

Father turned to him.

'Never mind, Tom,' he said. He meant because Tom was still only seventeen, and too young to enlist for almost another year. 'You can still go to Officer Training Corps and then you'll be ready. Maybe the war will still be on.'

'Father!' Edgar exclaimed. 'Don't talk nonsense. That's the sort of rot the pacifists spout.'

Father didn't like being spoken to like that, not even by Edgar.

'Edgar,' he said, tersely. 'I am simply trying to keep Tom's chin up. It's a shame for him to miss out when you'll be away fighting.'

Edgar glanced at Tom.

'He wouldn't go, anyway,' he snarled. 'He's only too glad he's too young.'

'What do you mean?' Father said.

'Just what I say.'

'That's an unkind . . .' Father began, but Tom interrupted him.

'It's true,' he said.

That stopped us all for a moment. It was the first time he'd spoken.

'What?' Father spluttered. 'You're not falling for all this Socialist nonsense, are you? I won't have a pacifist in my house!'

'No, Father,' Tom said. I could see he was scared of Father. 'No,' he said. 'I'm not a pacifist. But I don't want to fight.'

Father tried to interrupt, but Tom was brave enough to keep talking.

'I want to train to be a doctor,' he said. 'Like you.'

What could Father say to that? He calmed down a bit.

'That's a good thing, Thomas,' he said. 'A good thing. But there's a war on now. If the occasion arises for you to do your bit, then you must! You will go and fight.'

He seemed to think that was an end to the matter, but I, for some unknown reason, decided to speak.

'Why should he go and fight,' I said, 'if he doesn't want to?'

Edgar turned on me.

'Stupid girl! You don't understand anything about it. Don't interfere.'

I wasn't surprised. Edgar says things like that to me. If he says anything to me at all, that is, these days.

I could feel my face flushing red.

'I only let you stay here because I expect you not to speak,' Father said. 'You don't understand these matters. That's all there is to it.'

He sent me to my room. Tom forced a smile as I went, but I could hear their row go on as I went upstairs anyway.

I shut myself away, and stared out to sea. I suppose I should have been hurt by Edgar, and Father, but I'm used to their ways. That's just how Father is, with everyone in the house. Not just me. Mother too. I wonder sometimes what she was like when they got married, but I can't picture it. I only know her as she is now, at Father's beck and call. But I know he loves us, really, I know he does. And Edgar, well, it's simply that it's not that long since we were children, and we had fun, sometimes. It's just sad it's not like that anymore. We've all crossed a line; it has to happen sooner or later. Even Tom and me. I know I'll never be as close to him as when we were children, however much I try.

I stared out to sea. I could half see my reflection on the glass, and half the world outside. Across the waves, not so very far, I could imagine France. Everyone I knew was excited about the war, everyone in town, and we heard later there had been mass celebrations in London, in Trafalgar Square.

I looked across the water to France, and felt like the only person in the world who thought the war was a bad thing. That only bad things would come of it.

As I came down to breakfast this morning I heard my parents talking. I was late. Mother had let me sleep in after the business with the accident.

Something made me wait awhile on the darkness of the stairs. I gripped the mahogany banister tightly, feeling its familiar smooth, dark surface under my touch. I remember sitting there as a child, watching Cook and the previous maid going about their business. I'm far too tall to sit on the stairs any more, though somehow I'd still like to. Then I heard Mother say something about the tram.

'Nonsense!' Father said, loud enough for me to hear clearly.

Quickly I moved down to the bottom of the stairs, my hand hovered by the dining room door handle. I knew if I went in they would stop talking.

'But Henry,' she said, 'what if we *had* got on? We might have been desperately injured. Even killed.'

I didn't hear Father's reply.

'Well you explain it then,' Mother said.

'I don't need to because it's ridiculous.'

Suddenly I heard Father walking to the door. It sprung open.

'Alexandra!' he snapped. 'Always watching, always prying!'

He plucked his coat and hat from the stand and went off to work.

'Father, wait!'

He had left his armband behind.

As soon as the war started he had been sworn in as a special constable of the Brighton Borough Police. He is Special Constable No. 111 of the A Division. He goes patrolling the streets two or three nights a week. What he is patrolling for, I don't know, but he has to wear an armband to show his status.

He looked at me and took the armband.

'See if your mother needs help,' he said.

'With what?' I asked, quietly. The door was already shut.

What with being a special constable and his work, he is hardly at home these days. The New Grammar School was only open for a year before the war turned it into the Dyke Road Hospital, which Father now runs. St Mark's is another school that's been turned into a hospital for our soldiers. They have even turned the Pavilion into one for wounded Indians! It was the King's idea; perhaps he thought it would make them feel more at home.

In the evening, while Father was still patrolling, I tried to talk to Mother, while she sat doing some needlework.

'Mother,' I said, 'are you all right, now?'

She stopped what she was doing and looked at me.

'What do you mean, Sasha?' she asked, smiling.

'After the accident,' I said. 'I thought . . .'

Her smile disappeared.

'We weren't hurt, were we. Whatever do you mean?'

'I know we weren't hurt, but it was such a shock.'

She looked away.

'Yes,' she said, 'we had a lucky escape. If you hadn't . . .'
She paused.

'What?' I asked.

She didn't answer, so I tried again.

'What? If I hadn't told you I didn't want to get on the tram? Is that what you mean?'

'I'm busy, Alexandra. Don't pester me.'

I tried to press her, but the moment was lost. I wasn't Sasha anymore, I was Alexandra. But I wouldn't let it drop.

'That's it, isn't it?' I said. 'That's what's bothering you. How did I know we shouldn't get on the tram?'

'That's enough!' she said. 'You didn't *know* we shouldn't get on. I decided not to. We had a lucky escape. That's all.'

'But I knew!' I insisted. 'I knew.'

'Don't be ridiculous,' she shouted, with sudden anger. 'Now go to bed before your father gets home.'

I was so amazed that she'd shouted at me that momentarily I stood motionless, then ran upstairs.

My room, like the sitting room, has a clear view of the sea, even from the bed. It's the most wonderful thing I have, my view. I can see across the little gardens that belong to the whole street, then away over town to the sea itself. When we moved into Clifton Terrace I begged to have the room in the attic so I could see the sea, and though Edgar and Tom protested, I got my wish. I think it was the only time I ever made a fuss as a child. So Molly and Cook live in the basement, Mother and Father and my brothers share the house proper.

I sat on my bed, and wondered. I wondered about the war, and what it was doing to people. But can I really blame the war for the arguments between Father and Edgar, and Tom? Or for

Mother shouting at me? Or are those things there anyway, but just not seen until now? I don't know, but I want my family to be well.

Night waves washed along the summer shore, like a gentle thunder in some show of pretending. I gazed across the sea to the real night horizon, and felt the storms over the water. I knew the thunder rolling across the fields of France was no pretence.

*I*t was a bright and bone-chilling day today, a sign that winter is not so far away.

I went out for the first time since the accident. A piercing wind sailed in off the sea and up Ship Street as I went down to the seafront. It cut right through me even though Mother made me put on my warmest overcoat.

It was on another sunny day, though a warm August one, that Edgar went away to join the army. He decided to put his training to become a lawyer on hold, and didn't go back to Oxford that autumn. Instead, Father made some 'phone calls, and just as he said, Edgar got a commission. He had been on OTC camp; he had been to a good school. The army was eager to have him. He spent a couple of months at the regimental depot, learning to drill and be drilled, and whatever else officers need to know.

For a while he wrote to us, complaining that the war would be done before he had even started, but he need not have worried. The news from France was bad. There was a miserable article in *The Sunday Times* about heavy British losses, and the general invincibility of the German army. Even though the war had really only just begun, it had become a dreadful stalemate, and wounded were arriving in Folkestone and Harwich every day.

They had said it would all be over by Christmas, but Christmas came and went, and the war stayed. In the new year Edgar got the posting he had been waiting for, and went to France. Since then most of another year has come and gone, and still there is nothing but the war.

On many occasions I've asked Father if I might help in the hospital, but he refuses. He says nursing is no occupation for a girl from a respectable family. If the truth be told he doesn't think I should have any occupation at all, but just wait for someone of the right sort to marry me. The 'right sort' means rich, and from a good family. But I want to do something. I think I really do want to be a nurse. It goes way back to when I was tiny. I always wanted to help people, but I couldn't. When you're a little girl no one takes you seriously. You're not allowed to help people.

People like Clare.

I was only trying to help, but no one would listen. Somehow it's put a wall between me and my family, a wall of guilt and fear. J184,239

I've grown up now, and I still want to nurse. Edgar is mean to me about it. Ever since I was little he teased me, saying I would be scared, and that I would faint as soon as I saw blood. Then Tom would tell him to shut up and they'd start to fight instead, until I would cry and that stopped them both.

But I think things may have changed, because I heard Mother and Father talking this evening after they'd gone to bed. I can often hear them from my room. I don't think they realise how thin the ceiling and floor is between their bedroom and mine.

I stopped brushing my hair and bent down to the floor, pressing my ear against the boards.

'She's quite a young woman now,' I heard Mother say. 'She's pretty, but she's even more intelligent. And she's seventeen. You know she wants to do something.'

'It's still not the sort of thing she should be doing,' Father replied. 'You don't know what they're like, Dorothy. They're a rough bunch of girls.'

He meant the nurses in his hospital.

'Perhaps,' Mother said, 'but they do the job that needs doing. And things are changing. The war is changing things.'

'Don't preach to me about my own profession,' Father said, curtly. 'If Alexandra becomes a nurse you know the sort of people she'll have to deal with.'

'She could join the Women's Emergency Corps. That's only for decent women to join. The uniform alone costs two pounds.'

Father snorted.

'If by "decent women" you mean suffragettes . . .'

'Well, she'll have to do something. Sending her to Miss Garrett's for private tuition is all very well for now, but what then? You know what she's like. All that sitting, watching. She should have something to occupy her.'

'Are you talking about Alexandra now? Or do you mean to bring up your own complaints again . . . ?'

'No, Henry, no,' Mother said, quickly. 'You know I'm content. Really. But Alexandra should have something to do.'

'Maybe,' Father said. 'We'll see.'

'And she's always wanted to be a nurse.'

'And you know why!' Father said, suddenly raising his voice. 'You know when it started!'

Mother hushed him and their voices fell quiet, so that I couldn't hear any more.

I was very excited by what I'd heard. I couldn't sleep for a long time, but when I did I dreamt of playing with Clare in that summer garden, where she was alive once again.

Last Easter, about six months ago, Edgar came home on leave. We sat around the dining table at Sunday lunch, just as we always had, but something was not the same.

Although he'd been away for just a few months, Mother stared at him as if she'd never seen him before. He looked very smart in his captain's uniform, it was true.

'Well, my boy,' Father said, beaming. 'Tell us about the army.'

Tom pulled a face, which only I saw.

'Actually, it's been a pretty dull show,' Edgar said. He couldn't hide his disappointment. 'We've been in reserve, mostly. And the other officers . . . I get a hard time because I'm a special reserve captain.'

'Never mind,' Mother said, smiling. 'You're doing your best.'

Father nodded.

'Your chance will come,' he said.

'Yes, you're right,' Edgar said. 'And you'll get your chance too, Tom, after all. You'll be eighteen in July.'

We all looked at Tom.

'Well, Thomas?' Father said. 'Edgar's right.'

'I want to be a doctor,' he said, slowly.

*

That afternoon, we went out for a stroll along the seafront, past the West Pier, and along to Brunswick Lawns. What a fine, proud family we must have looked. Mother and Father arm in arm. Father was well known, and respected, and men nodded to him as we walked, with his children behind, me in the middle, Tom on the right and Edgar on the left, in his uniform.

The lawns were very busy, though before the war they would have been packed on a fine afternoon, and the ladies' clothes much more flamboyant. We passed a family we knew, with their invalid son in a chair. Father had treated the boy for many years, though without much success. His father smiled as we passed.

'What a fine daughter you have, now, Mrs Fox!' he said, and Mother smiled, but I thought about their son. I looked away.

The sun shone and gulls cried overhead, when suddenly, I saw a flash of colour at our side. I looked round to see a young woman in a dark blue dress approaching us. She had two friends with her, girls a little older than me, also in expensive dresses. Before we even knew what was happening, the girl was talking to Tom.

She was very pretty and at first Tom smiled as she pressed something into his hand.

Tom looked down at what she'd given him and his face fell. It was a white feather.

The girl muttered something and hurried off to rejoin her friends.

'But I'm not even eighteen yet,' Tom protested as she went.

We went home straight away, and no one said a word.

*W*hen we got in there was an awful row.

Edgar didn't even have to say anything. The look on his face was enough to tell Tom what he was thinking.

'The disgrace!' Father snorted.

'But I'm not even eighteen,' Tom said, again and again. 'Why didn't any of you tell them that?'

'But it's true!' Edgar said. 'You don't want to go to war. It doesn't matter what age you are or aren't. There's a name for people like you!'

'Edgar!' Mother cried. 'Stop it.'

She tried to stop everyone fighting, but it was no use. I stood beside her, watching, and without realising it, held her hand.

'It'll only get worse,' Father said. 'The older you get. When people know. You have to do your bit.'

'Is that all you can ever say?' Tom shouted at Father. I shuddered. None of us had ever raised our voice to him, but strangely, Father let it pass.

'That's all that counts,' he said.

'What?' asked Tom. 'Going to war? Killing?'

'Not killing,' Edgar said. 'Doing your bit. 'That's all. Fighting for what's right.'

'You haven't even done any fighting,' Tom spat at Edgar.

That really upset him. He stormed over to Tom, and for a moment they looked like they did when they were young boys; Tom trying to stand up to Edgar, even though he is five years younger, and so much weaker.

'That's not my fault,' Edgar shouted. 'And when I get the chance, I'll fight. I'm no coward!'

'Is that what you think I am?' Tom said, angrily.

Maybe Edgar hadn't meant that. I don't think he did, but now the word was spoken, it seemed impossible he could take it back.

'Yes. Coward.'

Tom stood, rigid, his face drained, his teeth clenched. He took a deep breath.

'All I want to do,' he said finally, 'is to go to medical school. I'd rather save men here than kill them over there.'

He stepped past Edgar, and avoiding Father's eyes, made his way upstairs as calmly as he could.

When we were children, my brothers would often fight, and sometimes I'd get involved too. We fought about little things, as children do, and sometimes Tom and Edgar would fight because Edgar had been mean to me. It seemed deadly at the time, but we all grew up, and the years between Edgar and Tom and me began to tell. The two of them bickered instead of punched, and while Tom and I were still close as we got older, Edgar grew distant, and paid me no attention.

The argument over the white feather reminded me of all that. I was watching, just the same. Except now we were fighting about something truly deadly.

That was six months ago, the Easter of 1915.

Such a lot has changed since then. Edgar went back to the war, and got his wish. He wrote to us that his battalion was being called up from reserve and would soon see real action. Mother is very worried, but tries not to show it. Father is proud.

Tom has gone, though not to the war as Father and Edgar want him to. He went to Manchester to study medicine.

I miss him. My brother who is almost a twin to me, although there is a year between us.

But something good has happened. I don't know why, but

Father has finally agreed to let me spend some time on the wards at the Dyke Road Hospital, to see if I want to go into nursing properly.

I am very excited; this is my chance to show everyone that I can be useful, that I can help people.

Tomorrow, I will see what the future has in store for me.

'Sister Cave will take you round,' Father said. 'Stick next to her. Don't say anything unless she asks you a question, and do everything she tells you to. And don't get in anyone's way.'

He walked away down the dimly-lit corridor that leads to his office.

Sister's about my mother's age I suppose, and quite friendly, but I felt nervous because of Father's attitude. If anything were to go wrong he'd never let me come back.

We pushed through the half-glass doors and were in the ward.

'Wait here while I get the trolley,' Sister said.

Ahead of me I could see the beds, but it was nothing like a normal hospital ward. The building had been built as the new boys' school only two years ago, but as soon as the war had started it had been commandeered as a military hospital. In this makeshift arrangement, the beds are crushed in tight together, trying to make as much use of the space as possible.

It was all very quiet. I don't know what I'd been expecting but I was surprised that there wasn't more noise. I took a couple of steps forward, and noticed another room opposite the one Sister had gone into.

The door was open. Something made me take another step

and I saw a man in pyjamas sitting on a wooden chair. He was young, but had thinning hair.

He gazed intently ahead, but when I moved further to see what he was looking at, I saw nothing but a blank white wall.

I jumped as I heard a clatter behind me, and turned to see Sister wheeling the trolley towards me.

'Right, Alexandra. Or should I be calling you "Nurse", now?'

I smiled and looked back at the man in the white room, a question on my lips.

Sister came over.

'Him?' she said. 'Mental case.'

She said it loud enough for him to have heard, but he showed no sign of having done so.

'Nothing we can do for him.'

She emphasised the word 'we'.

'Doesn't he do anything?' I asked. 'Say anything?'

'Occasionally,' she said. 'But it's all nonsense.'

'What's his name?'

She looked at a chart by the door.

'Evans,' she said. 'David. Welsh. Heaven knows how he ended up here.'

She moved off with the trolley, and I followed.

We went from bed to bed, and Sister dispensed medication to some of the men. She gave morphia to those in pain, but for many there was nothing to do.

Then came a moment I had been dreading.

'We need to change this dressing,' Sister said.

I looked down at the man in the bed. He was at least twice my age, and I felt my lip tremble. He was only half awake, but as Sister pulled back his sheets, he hissed in pain and his eyes shot open.

'We'll be as fast as we can,' Sister told him, and he nodded. His face showed no expression at all.

The wound was in his thigh, and Sister deftly cut off the old dressing and dropped it into a metal bin underneath the trolley.

'Good,' she said. 'No need to inflict iodine on you today.'

She smiled at the man, then turned to me.

'Pass me that one,' she said.

I handed her the clean dressing, and she bandaged his thigh up again. She moved so rapidly I barely had time to realise how disgusting the wound was, how there was no muscle where there should have been.

Everything was going well, and I felt proud of myself, though I was still nervous.

Then it all went wrong.

We came to the last bed.

The man who lay there was younger than all the others.

Sister smiled.

'Not much to do here, either,' she said. 'He's nearly better. Gas case. His eyes and lungs were damaged, but he's on the mend. Be back in France before he knows it.'

'Where's Nurse Gallagher today then, Sister?' the man asked.

'You've got me today. And this is Alexandra. She's a special visitor, I'm showing her the ropes. You can be my guinea-pig.'

'Lungs,' Sister said. 'And look. Take a close look at his eyes. Can you see the inflammation of the tear ducts?'

I leant right up to the man and peered into his eyes.

'Of course, it was much worse; nearly better now.'

That was the last thing I heard Sister saying.

I looked into the man's eyes, but I didn't see inflamed tear ducts. I saw an empty bed. I saw death.

I think I began to shake, and then I heard the man speak.

'My God,' he said. 'My God. Her eyes!'

He tried to back away from me, squirming in the bed.

'Her eyes!' he shouted again, and other patients began to call out from their beds.

Then he began to cough and choke.

'What does he mean?' I asked. 'What's wrong with . . . ?'

'There's nothing wrong with you,' Sister said quickly, 'but you'd better go home. I'll tell your father.'

'No!' I cried.

'Don't worry, it's not your fault. Go on.'

She turned to soothe the man who still lay hacking and coughing in bed.

As I went I took a last look, and saw him staring back at me.

I was too far away to hear him, but I could read his lips.

'Her eyes!'

It's late now and I'm in bed.

I didn't have long to wait until Father arrived home. He came up to my room.

'I heard there was some trouble,' he said, standing in the doorway.

'It wasn't anything to do with me,' I began to protest, but he held up his hand.

'I didn't say it was. The hospital is full of damaged men, Alexandra. Sometimes it's not their bodies that are damaged.'

I nodded.

'Is he all right?' I asked.

'Physically, yes. He'll be home in a week.'

I said nothing. Nothing of what I have been thinking.

Father took a step into the room.

'You did well, today,' he said.

'That man, you're sure he's going to be all right?'

'Absolutely,' Father said. 'But you must understand. If you want to be a nurse, you'll see plenty more men who won't be.'

I have tried to sleep but I cannot.

Father says the man is all right, Sister said so too, but I know that he is about to die.

I know it.

And there is something else. There is what he said about my eyes. I have spent all evening looking at myself in my looking-glass. I can see my long dark hair, the white skin of my face, and the redness of my lips, but in my dark eyes I see nothing.

Nothing.

*S*omething is happening to me.

I knew immediately that man is going to die. I didn't see anything specific, just a bed emptied of its body, a body emptied of its life.

I have waited all day for Father to get home from work. I need to ask him, yet I dread asking, because I already know the answer. But I forgot that he was patrolling as a special constable this evening, so he won't be home for another few hours, yet.

Something is happening to me that I don't understand. And yet it's becoming clearer.

Clare.

When I saw what was going to happen to Clare, I was only five. What form do a five-year-old's thoughts take? I spoke then without hesitation, without self-awareness. I said what was in my head.

With George, Edgar's friend, well, that was just a dream. With the soldier on the tram, it was a sensation, but I didn't really know what I was feeling. But in the ward yesterday, I started to see something, a vision of death, and the knowledge of exactly what it meant.

And if I saw something, then so had he. He saw something in my eyes that made him very scared.

If I can see the future, then what does that mean? It would be like knowing the end of a story right from the start, almost as if you were reading it backwards.

And who wants to know how their own story ends?

*T*hree days have passed since Father came home and told me he was dead.

His name was John Simpson. Each day I would ask how he was and Father told me he was fine.

'Are you trying to be a diligent nurse?' he asked, taking off his coat, and hanging it in the hall. 'Is that it?'

I shrugged, but next day when I asked, he was angry, and told me I was not a nurse in his hospital, not yet, and that I ought to spend more time supporting Mother, whatever that means. What does she need support with? She's not allowed to do anything.

When he came home on the third day, the first thing he saw was me, waiting in the hallway.

He had a very grim look on his face, and I was scared, but not really of his anger.

He made to walk past me to the drawing room, but I stood in front of him.

'How is he?'

Father glared at me.

I followed him into the drawing room.

'Simpson,' I said. 'How is he?'

'Alexandra, leave it be!' Father shouted. 'You are obsessed!'

I had my answer.

'He's dead, isn't he?'

The words tumbled from my mouth.

I had my answer. Later I learnt that a pneumonic infection had set in suddenly, and with his lungs in a weakened state, Simpson had died rapidly.

'Why are you cross with me?' I asked Father. 'It's not my fault!'

'Of course it isn't,' he shouted. With that Mother came running into the room.

'But why do you think I kept asking about him?' I asked. I turned to Mother. 'You know I kept asking about him!'

She looked from me to Father, then went and held his arm to calm him down.

'But I knew it was going to happen,' I said. 'I knew.'

'You knew nothing,' Father said. I could see he was tired as well as angry. 'You are a silly girl who is too sensitive to be a nurse. A man has died, Alexandra! Show some respect. Please – go to your room.'

So I went, and I was only halfway up the stairs when I realised I had been foolish to say anything. They don't want to talk about it, and now Father will probably stop me from visiting the hospital again.

I was stupid to say anything, but I could not help myself.

I am scared.

I have seen the future four times, and each time the future has been death.

*I*t is November, 1915.

The war continues, with no sign that it will end before this, or any other Christmas. It's like an avalanche, started by a single gunshot, but which roars down the mountain more loudly than a thousand cannons. Every day there is some new complication, some new engagement, some new political battle. I don't understand much of it, but it seems to me there is no way of stopping the avalanche.

Even so there's some better news. Edgar wrote a few days ago and thinks he will be getting leave soon. It will be good to see him and will put Mother's mind at rest, too. To have one of my brothers back at home for a few days might make things seem more normal. The house is very quiet without either of them around. Tom writes almost every other day from Manchester. I am so proud of him for doing what he thinks is right, but I know it has been hard.

He says he has been white-feathered again in the street. When Father read that part of the letter he grunted and wouldn't read the rest, though Mother and I did, later.

I only hope he gets to finish his training. There has been talk in the newspapers that the government might introduce conscription, and then that would be that. Tom would have to join the army whether he wanted to or not. But maybe he could join the Medical Corps so he could at least keep on being a doctor.

I have been studying as usual, visiting Miss Garrett's house with the three other girls who attend her private lessons. And I have been trying to persuade Father to take me back to the hospital. So far he refuses to discuss it, though he himself said I did well on my first day there.

I know what he is afraid of.

*E*dgar doesn't write much. The last time was to tell us about his leave, but he did say that his battalion had seen action at last.

Father read the letter out loud to Mother and me at breakfast. Edgar is a captain. He is twenty-four. These two things seem not to belong together, but they are true. He has a company of men to command.

'I'll write to Thomas,' Mother said.

'What for?' Father asked, looking up from Edgar's letter.

'To see if he can come home. When Edgar does.'

'What for?' Father asked again.

'Because it will be nice for us all to be together.'

Father put down Edgar's letter and took up the paper instead.

'The boys will want to see each other, anyway,' Mother continued. 'We ought to try and be together as a family when we can.'

Father snorted.

'We won't know when he's coming, anyway,' he said. 'We may not get any warning at all, so you won't be able to tell Thomas when to come.'

'Well,' said Mother, 'we'll see. Maybe Edgar will be able to let us know.'

41

'He won't,' Father said.

Mother put down her teacup with a rattle in its saucer.

'And maybe he will,' she blurted out. I looked up at Father who had dropped the paper and stared at Mother. He got up and left the room without another word.

Mother stood up too when he had gone, without even calling Molly to clear the things away. I heard her open the back door and go into the garden. I stared at the tablecloth, a blue gingham check. I noticed all the tiny crumbs from my toast lying on it, and then I noticed fat tears dropping on to them from my eyes.

I knew why Mother was upset, and I felt it too.

I sat by myself at the table.

I tried to talk to Mother.

I couldn't get Father even to listen to me.

But they don't know what I feel, what I have felt each time it has happened. What I have felt is just as real to me as any other feeling or emotion that I might have at any point in any day.

How can I make them understand?

There is no one I can talk to about this. Mother won't listen to me, because she loves me too much. To her I'll always be Sasha, her little princess. I know she thinks I should be allowed to do something with my life, but she's scared of losing me, and too cowed by Father to help me do anything about it.

Maybe I could talk to Thomas, but he's not here anymore. He's got a scientific mind, that's why he'll be a good doctor, but he's open-minded too. I know he'd listen to me at least. I wouldn't even try to talk to Edgar.

Maybe I could talk to Miss Garrett about it. I'm not sure it's wise. I certainly wouldn't talk to the other girls in her class. They're so silly, and just spend their time gossiping and giggling. And one or two odd things have been happening to me there, as well.

Small things, chance occurrences, coincidences.

In Miss Garrett's lessons we have been studying *The Iliad*, the story of Troy. Of Helen and Paris, of Agamemnon and Clytemnestra. Today Miss Garrett broke off from her discussion of the death of Achilles and began to tell us about something else. She was very animated and engaging as she spoke of the recurrent symbols of myth.

Miss Garrett is amazing. She's not that young, and despite the fact that she is quite beautiful, she has not married yet. She went to university and has been teaching privately ever since. She has such energy in what she does. I want to do the same with nursing.

She was talking about specific symbolic meanings, and as she did, I knew just what she was about to say, before she had said it. And as I felt this, I remembered a dream from last night, a vivid dream, which I had quite forgotten until this afternoon.

'I mention this,' Miss Garrett was saying, 'because we have been looking at the battles before the walls of Troy. Such dramatic events as these in human history of course give rise to many striking thoughts and images.'

It was a strange feeling, and not a nice one, to hear her talk. To hear her say exactly what I knew she was going to say, just a moment or so before the words actually left her lips.

'One such symbol, that occurs in many mythologies, including the Greek, the Celtic and the Norse, is that of the raven. It has become a symbol of the battlefield, a harbinger of ill-omen and death. Why? Because the raven is a carrion bird, and would have flocked to feed on the corpses of the Greek and Trojan warriors.'

The raven.

That was my dream.

I saw a raven swooping down towards my face, all black beak

and claws and feathers. The bird clawed at my face, and I felt its feathers brush my hair, smelt their mustiness. It came back to me so strongly as I sat there that I was unaware of anything else, and even Miss Garrett's words came to me as if over a great distance. This is hard to explain, but I felt as unreal as if I was a figure in a photograph, in black and white, not a real person at all.

I suffered a terrible sense of isolation and though there were four other people in the room, I felt utterly alone.

As I was leaving Miss Garrett's yesterday I asked her if I could borrow a copy of *The Iliad*.

She looked a bit surprised.

'I didn't think you were interested,' she said coldly. 'You appeared rather distracted in class.'

'Miss?' I said, not knowing what to say.

She shrugged.

'Could you lend me a copy, please?' I asked again. 'I would like to do some more reading.'

I don't think she believed me entirely, but she agreed.

After the other girls had gone she led me into a different room, one I have never seen before. Every single inch of wall was lined with bookshelves. Only the windows and the fireplace were not devoted to books. She pulled the curtains to let in some more light and began scanning the shelves.

'The primers we use in class are a little dry. They miss out on so much,' Miss Garrett was saying.

She stood on a small stool and pulled a book from a high shelf.

'Here we are,' she said. 'This was my copy when I was your age. You can borrow it.'

She handed me the book.

'There's not just *The Iliad* in there. There're many other stories from the Greek myths too. I hope you will enjoy it.'

I nodded.

'I'll take good care of it,' I said, and she smiled.

I got home a little while ago.

I thought about the dozens, in fact hundreds, of books, on her shelves, and felt proud that she was happy for me to take the little leather-bound edition that belonged to her.

I've been reading it in bed, but I don't know quite what for. I thought I was looking for something, but I realise now I just wanted to read a good story, to escape from everything that's been happening in my head. The stories are full of deaths, awful deaths, and battles and tragedy; but somehow it's comforting. It reminds me that what's going on, what Edgar's been seeing, is not so unusual. And that reminds me that one day, things will be normal again. Things will be all right, if we all try hard enough to make them that way.

85

*E*dgar came home yesterday, and just as Father said, there was no warning of his arrival. The first we knew was when he sent a telegram from Folkestone to say he was about to catch a train to Brighton. Even if we got in touch with Tom now, by the time he gets here Edgar may have gone again.

As much as Mother wants her family to be together again, a part of me thinks that maybe it's for the best, really.

It was very late when Edgar arrived. Mother said I couldn't wait up any longer and sent me to bed, but of course I couldn't sleep. I heard him arrive eventually, sometime after midnight, because the clock in the hall had already struck twelve a while before. I heard Mother's voice, high with excitement but not loud, and then Edgar and Father's voices, deep and quiet.

He went to bed after just a few words – I heard him come up the stairs. He went along the landing on the floor below me to the bathroom. I don't know why but something felt different. He had already been away to war and home on leave once, so why it wasn't the same this time I had no idea.

I wanted to see him, but I hesitated. I listened as he came out of the bathroom and back to his old room again, and though I knew Mother would be cross, I crept out of my room and looked down the stairs to the landing.

'Edgar!' I whispered, waving a hand.

He jumped and turned suddenly at his door in the dark hallway. I heard him breathing, softly.

'Oh, Alexandra,' he said, looking up the stairs. 'It's you. Go back to bed.'

His voice was flat, and his eyes wouldn't fix on me.

'I'll see you in the morning,' I said, trying to sound cheerful, but his door was already shut behind him. I stood by myself, then went back to my room.

I lay awake, listening to the noises of the house. Boards creaking and the November wind rustling the empty branches of the magnolia beneath my window, brushing fallen leaves along the high pavement of Clifton Terrace. I could sense my parents and Edgar asleep in their rooms, lost in their own dreams, and though Thomas was missing, it felt almost normal.

I didn't see Edgar this morning. I woke with my head full of dark clouds, struggling to rouse myself after a sleepless night. I think it was quite early when I finally dropped off. By the time I got downstairs Edgar had gone out.

'I hardly saw him myself,' Mother said. There was something in her voice I couldn't quite place. She wasn't cross with him, but I think she expected to have her son all to herself once he was home.

'Where's he gone?' I asked.

'He's gone for a walk,' she said, as if it were a crime.

'He probably just wants some air,' I said. 'Have a look at the town, you know. To make himself feel at home again.'

'On a day like this?' Mother asked.

She looked out of the window. It was a bleak morning, with rain slanting across the houses on the way down to the sea, and across the water itself, in great grey swathes. It was no morning to be taking a casual stroll.

Lunchtime came and went. It's Sunday and Mother asked Cook to make a proper Sunday lunch. We've had to skimp recently on those kind of things, and today she wanted it done properly, but Edgar still hadn't returned.

Father, Mother and I ate lunch without him, in the end, though much of it was cold.

'That was lovely,' Father said, without smiling. 'Thank you, dear.'

It was suppertime before Edgar came back.

Not a word was said about where he'd been, or that he'd missed lunch. We all pretended nothing had happened and sat down for some bread, cheese and cold meat. Father opened a bottle of beer for Edgar and one for himself. I watched as the beautiful dark brown liquid frothed into the glasses, making such a lovely comforting sound as it did. The clock on the wall ticked, very slowly.

'So,' said Father, 'tell us what you've been up to.'

I looked at Edgar, who was staring at his plate, and methodically pushing food into his mouth. It was clear to me he didn't want to talk about anything.

But Father was quite unaware that anything was wrong.

'What's been happening in your section? Much action? I expect you've shown the enemy a thing or two.'

'There's not much to tell,' Edgar said, and took another slice of bread. 'We're doing our bit, you know.'

'But you must have seen a sight or two,' Father went on. 'Tell us something.'

'Yes,' Edgar said, 'we've seen a sight or two. Now, if you'll excuse me, I think I ought to go to bed.'

He got up. Father frowned.

'But . . .'

'Henry,' Mother cut in. 'He's tired. Let him sleep.'

I was surprised at Mother's boldness, and looked sharply at

Father to see his reaction, but he just sighed and went off to the drawing room to read by the fire.

I stayed with Mother while Molly flapped around us, clearing away. When it was done, we sat together for a while.

'Why?' I asked Mother quietly.

'Why what, Sasha?' she said.

I felt how tired she was, could hear the sick weariness in her voice, but I couldn't stop myself.

'Why won't you believe me? Why won't anyone believe me?'

I wished I hadn't said it.

Mother came round the table and put her arms around me.

'Please don't, Sasha,' she said. 'Please stop saying it. Please.'

She put her face in my hair and began to shake and then I realised she was crying.

I stood up and held her.

'I'm sorry,' I said. 'I'm sorry, I don't want to upset you.'

She said nothing for a while, but then stood back from me, wiping her eyes.

She was about to speak when we were interrupted.

'Will there be anything else, tonight, Ma'am?' Molly asked from the doorway.

Mother shook her head.

'No, thank you, Molly. Alexandra is just going to bed. We shall follow shortly.'

I tried to hold Mother's eyes, but she would not return my gaze. I went upstairs.

It's always the same. I'm their dutiful daughter. That's who they want me to be. And if I show the slightest sign of being difficult or strange they simply won't accept it. How I long to do something! If not, then it would be better to have been

Clare; for my life to have finished before I did anything to upset anyone.

I got to sleep quite quickly for once, but I woke suddenly. I heard noises from Edgar's room, the sound of talking. Then I realised it was just one voice. Edgar's. He was calling out in his sleep. Crying out.

Some of it sounded like people's names, but much of it was incomprehensible.

Then he began to whimper, like a beaten dog. It went on and on, then stopped. It started again, not so loud, and stopped again.

I think he's sleeping more peacefully now, but I'm wide awake.

What sights has Edgar seen to make noises like that?

83

*E*dgar has gone back to France, sadly before Thomas even knew he was in the country. It's a shame because Christmas is coming and at Christmas a family ought to be together.

Edgar left a day early, too. He said in his telegram that he had six days, but he was gone by Wednesday morning. If I'm honest, though, it was a bit difficult anyway. Mother would be furious with me for saying something like that, but it's true. Edgar spent much of the time out of the house, who knows where, as if he were an animal that didn't like being locked up. When he was at home he was silent for the most part. Mother kept on smiling and having Cook put food in front of him. Father did all the talking, and spoke about the war and the army, while Edgar sat staring into the fire, clutching a glass of beer in his big hands.

I did nothing, but simply sat and watched it all, pretending to read Miss Garrett's *Greek Myths*. Though I showed nothing on the outside, inside I felt a sadness so strong it seemed to paralyse me.

It was strange that Edgar left early, as if he thought he would be more comfortable in France than he was here. I wondered what could make him feel like that.

When the time came for him to leave Father said he would

walk with him to the station, but he forbade Mother and me to go. He said we would only get upset. I have walked past the station a hundred times and seen women saying goodbye to their men, some calm, but many with tears streaming down their faces. Father is probably right, we would have got upset. But I don't see what would be wrong with that.

So the moment came for Edgar to say goodbye, and it was a moment I had been fearing, in case . . .

In case I should feel something.

He gave Mother a kiss, and she smiled at him, but there were tears in her eyes.

He took a step towards me. I froze. Then, quite out of character, he put his arms around me and kissed me. It has been years since he has done that, since I was a child. I could feel him, strong and wiry under his smart uniform, and it was a surprise to me. And though he was home for five days and had a bath almost every day, I could smell the war on him still.

I could smell earth and things that I don't know the names of. A faint but clear aroma of something chemical that pricked the back of my nose; a smoky smell.

I could sense it all, but as my heart began to calm itself, I realised I could sense nothing of death.

I pulled away from Edgar, relieved, smiling.

'Have a good Christmas,' I said, and almost for the first time since he had returned, he laughed.

'Bless you, Alexandra,' he said, and then he went.

82

*A*t last I have been able to get back into the hospital. Father called me to see him a few days ago. It was quite late and he was obviously tired, but he seemed to want to talk there and then.

'You're still serious about this nursing business?' he said.

I was taken aback, briefly, but this was no time to appear vague or uncertain.

'Yes, Father,' I said. 'Yes. I really want to do it.'

'Very well, then. You may begin your training as a VAD nurse. You know what that is?'

I said I did. I'm seventeen, so it means I can work part-time in one of the hospitals, though I will live at home.

'You'll be among the youngest. There are Voluntary Aid Detachment nurses at my hospital. I've got you a place there, starting next week. But you'll have to fit this in around your studies, you understand that?'

'Yes, I do,' I said. 'Thank you!'

I smiled, from sheer happiness.

'Don't let me down, Alexandra, will you,' he said. There was no smile on his face.

'No,' I said. 'I promise.'

'Off you go then,' he said, as if I were ten years younger.

Automatically I turned to go, but then stopped. I had to know something.

I wondered if he had forgotten, or decided to ignore, the business with Simpson. Whatever else, I am pleased that nothing has happened since those three recent occasions when I saw the future. I hardly dare to think it, but maybe it has stopped. Things come in threes, after all.

'Father?' I said.

'What?'

'What made you change your mind? About me working in a hospital?'

'That's none of your concern,' he said.

'Isn't it?' I said. I was taking a big risk questioning him, but I thought it too odd to drop the subject.

He looked at me again, but I could read nothing from his face; as if he were a stranger to me.

'It was your brother,' he said, eventually.

'Thomas?' I asked.

'No, Edgar.'

'Edgar?' I spluttered, taken by surprise.

'When I walked him to the station, he said you ought to have your chance. He convinced me. So I'm giving you your chance.'

I smiled, my hand lingering on the brass door knob of Father's study.

'It's a good thing, Father,' I said. 'I believe I should have work to do.'

'He also said he didn't think you were up to it.'

He looked away out of the window.

The smile left my face and I left the room. As I closed the door behind me, I heard Father say one more thing.

'Prove him wrong.'

J spoke to Thomas on the telephone this evening, and Mother let me have almost the whole three minutes myself. Father didn't talk to him at all.

I told Thomas about Edgar's visit and what he had done for me.

'That's wonderful,' he said, but you wouldn't have thought so from the sound of his voice. There was a note of hesitation in it.

It's hard to tell what someone is really thinking on the 'phone, and I didn't really feel what Thomas was thinking. I could only feel the distance between us.

It's such a long way to Manchester. In fact, it's a funny thing, that Tom is farther away from us in Manchester than Edgar is, in France. But Edgar's not just in a different place, he's in a different world now, too.

*I*t was my first day as a VAD nurse today. I am only allowed to work part-time, but it's a big step forward from my few days' trial earlier in the autumn.

I walked to Seven Dials and carried on up Dyke Road. At the corner of the Old Shoreham Road the hospital stood waiting for me. It's a massive building, of red brick, with an elaborate sculpture on the portico above the entrance, and on top, a small cupola with a copper dolphin weathervane.

I stood for a moment, feeling scared, but then two girls brushed past me, laughing.

'You lost?' one of them asked.

'No,' I said. 'Well, a little. It's my first day.'

'Well, you don't look like a patient, that's for sure! You need to report to reception.'

Before half an hour had passed I was standing in my uniform outside Sister's office, waiting to be called in. The uniform felt strange, and itchy, but I was happy to be wearing it. It's a long grey dress, with full sleeves. Over the top I wear a white apron with a bold red cross.

Sister Maddox is not nice. She's a small, thin woman, maybe in her fifties, but I'm not sure, because I have tried not to look at her directly. She seemed hostile before I had even opened my mouth.

'Fox,' she said, 'you may only be a Voluntary Aid Detachment nurse and a part-timer at that, but in my hospital you will behave correctly. You will refer to me as Sister, and my nurses as Nurse such-and-such. You will not refer to VAD nurses by anything other than their surname, nor will you expect to be addressed in any other way yourself. Clear?'

I nodded. I didn't want to speak in case my voice sounded as scared as I felt.

'VADs are here to relieve the workload on my nurses – those who have proper medical training. And you are only here because of who your father is. Now, report to Staff-nurse Goodall.'

That was my introduction to the world of nursing, but I am determined not to let one horrible Sister spoil it. Later in the day, talking to other VAD nurses, I discovered that Sister Maddox hates all VADs, because we haven't had full medical training and yet are in demand. The soldiers call everyone 'Sister', out of friendliness, or politeness, or maybe just ignorance, when really they shouldn't, and that annoys her even more.

'So don't take it personally,' one girl said.

'But it is personal, with me,' I said.

'Oh, yes. Your father,' she said. 'But don't worry, most people around here like him. And they respect him, because he has hard work to do. He works on the neurasthenia patients.'

'The what?' I asked.

'Neurasthenia. The ones with shell-shock.'

I noticed that the corner of her mouth twisted slightly

as she said the word. She got on with her work, and I with mine.

It was a hard day, and by the time I got home this evening, I was ready to cry. Fortunately Father was working late. Mother seemed to realise I'd had a difficult day. She didn't question me about anything, just asked Molly to bring me my supper. Then she sat and talked to me.

'My first day, too,' she said, but I didn't understand. I felt guilty, because I could see Mother wanted to talk, but my head was full of the day, and I needed silence.

'What do you mean?' I asked, forcing myself to talk.

'My first day alone. Father at work. Edgar and Tom gone. And now you.'

'Mother, I . . .'

'It's all right, Sasha. I'm just saying. That's all.'

'You had Cook, and Molly.'

Mother dropped her voice.

'That's hardly the same,' she said, pulling a face.

In spite of myself, I laughed. I knew what she meant.

But my mind was still struggling through my day at the hospital.

'I'll get Molly to bring in your favourite supper. I've had her make an omelette for you.'

Any other day I would have been delighted. But I was just too tired.

I made an excuse and left Mother by herself in the dining room.

*

I came upstairs to bed, where I am now. I know it's selfish but I don't want to think about anyone else at the moment, not even Tom.

*T*here is so much to learn, but after half a dozen shifts at the hospital I'm no longer nervous each time I close those great front doors behind me. And I feel proud walking up the Dyke Road in my uniform.

As I pass women in the street, they smile, and some even say a word or two. Perhaps they have sons fighting in the war and I'm doing something to help. That means a lot.

This morning a postman standing in the doorway of a café whistled at me. Mother would have been appalled, but it made me smile. He meant no harm, and I marched into the hospital ready to face Maddox, or whatever else came my way. In my few days I have already seen some awful sights.

The worst are wounds to the face. A missing leg or arm is bad, that's true. It's terrible to think how that must feel, but at least you can still see that the patient is a person. But some facial wounds stop a man from looking human. There's a poor man in one bed who has a hole where his nose and mouth should be. He's covered in bandages, of course, but even that is wrong. There's no bump where his nose should be. His face is just a flat round ball of bandages, with a tube to feed him through. It's impossible not to wonder what will be there when the bandages come off. And somewhere he must have family, a wife or a brother. Certainly a mother and father, though no one has ever come to see him.

Despite these horrors, I am enjoying it at last. I know I have a more privileged background than many of the nurses here, but I am trying hard to be one of them. To be honest, it's very easy, because the work is hard and constant and we're all in it together. The main difference is something on the inside. The other nurses see the war differently, they see the soldiers differently.

'What brave men!' they'll say.

'Poor things.'

'We'll soon get them right, then they can go and sort them out!'

The Germans, they mean.

And they crow about our brave men. It's not that I don't think they're brave, it's simply that when I look at a broken body, all I feel is sadness. Not pride, or pity, or horror, or hatred. To me those are false feelings, emotions that we put on top of our sadness, because of the war, because of our country, or because we don't want to feel afraid.

I just wish it didn't have to be like this.

As I went to bed last night I saw the *Greek Myths* Miss Garrett loaned me when I went to her house. Guiltily I realised I have barely picked it up again since then, but I've been too busy by day, and too tired in the evening to think about reading.

Maybe there's another reason, too.

At first I read the stories greedily each night. They're so full of wonderful characters; heroes and heroines. Such awful things happen to them, it's easy to sympathise with them. I found myself wondering who I would be, if I were in the myths. And after a few nights I found my answer.

I read a few lines, just a very few lines, about a young girl from Troy, called Cassandra. A prophetess, who sees the future, and who no one believes.

Suddenly I found I didn't want to read the stories anymore, stories of people killing and loving and dying. There's too much of that going on all the time, as it is. I don't want these stories now, even though they were comforting before.

Thomas wrote to me today, which was wonderful.

I put his letter in my pocket, because I knew it would irritate Father if I read it at the breakfast table.

'Are you going to be at the hospital this afternoon?' Father said to me. 'I would like you to have tea with me. Four o'clock?'

'Yes,' I said, surprised.

So after I got back from Miss Garrett's I changed into my uniform and made my way up to the hospital.

I could tell Sister Maddox was not happy when I said I was to meet my father as soon as I reported for duty, but there wasn't much she could do about it. He's the doctor after all, and she's a sister. That's how things work.

When we got to Father's office on the second floor he wasn't there.

'Well, I suppose you'd better wait,' she said. 'Since you're his daughter I'm sure that will be fine.'

I looked around. I wondered why I had never visited him here before, but then there's a lot I don't know about my father. He doesn't talk much about his work when he's at home.

I soon got bored with waiting, and went over to the window with its views across town and down to the sea. It was as if I could feel something tugging at me again. From France, across the waves. It was stronger this time.

I was scared. I didn't want Father to see me like this.

I sat down at his desk and flicked through the papers on his desk, then realised what I was doing and stopped.

There was a book lying face down on his desk. *The Duality of the Mind* by Arthur Wigan. It looked very old. It was next to a sheaf of papers, the top one of which was much more recent, dated 1908, and called *Memory of the Present and False Recognition*, by someone called Bergson. I had a struggle to understand what the title meant, but it took my mind away from the window.

'Alexandra.'

Father was at the door.

I jumped up.

'I'm sorry I'm late. Sometimes it's hard to leave.'

He seemed distracted, but came and sat in the chair I had vacated.

'I've sent for some tea . . .'

'Were you doing rounds?' I asked.

'No,' he said. 'I don't do that kind of work here. I see . . . special cases.'

I nodded, and smiled, trying to show I knew what he meant. He didn't elaborate.

'Where's that confounded woman?' he said, looking out through the door. There was no sign of the tea.

'What exactly do you do, here?' I asked. He must have seen me looking at the papers on his desk.

'I'm doing tests,' he said. 'It's not easy to explain, but I'm involved with a group of doctors here. A lot of men are getting hurt in this war – badly hurt. But some of them aren't hurt in their bodies at all. Do you see?'

'I think so. Is that what they call shell-shock?'

'Shell-shock. *Shell-shock*,' he said, spitting the words out. 'Yes, that's what people call it. The group I work with here, we're doing tests to find out more about it. My colleagues are of the opinion that these men are as badly wounded as the fellows in the ward you work in.'

'But you don't agree?' I asked.

'No, I do not.'

He paused.

'I have no doubt that there are some cases who have severe mental illness, but the vast majority do not. Those that are ill were probably prone to it before they went to war. And the country needs every fit man to do his duty. To fight. We cannot bear the weight of malingerers.

'Where's that tea?' he said again, then turned to me. 'Well, look at you. My daughter is a nurse!'

I smiled.

'How is it? Are you sure it's what you want to do?'

'Yes,' I said. 'I'm sure. But I had better be going. Sister Maddox . . .'

He laughed, but without amusement.

'Yes, I see. Maybe you're right. Off you go, then. I'm sorry about the tea, but if Maddox gives you one word of trouble, you let me know.'

'Yes, Father,' I said, and went back down to the wards.

I have been working. I've been happy. It was almost as if I dreamt about what the future held, rather than it having happened. And the memory of a nightmare is much less frightening than the nightmare itself.

Then yesterday, the nightmare came back.

I was on the ward, making a bed. Without warning everything seemed unreal. I felt detached, like that time in Miss Garrett's lesson. My body felt like an empty shell.

Slowly, I turned my head, straightening up as I did so. It seemed to take forever to make that simple movement.

I realised that I had deliberately turned to look at a patient on the other side of the ward. He was talking to a nurse. I knew him. Shrapnel in the back of his head and shoulders.

'You'll be out of here, soon,' the nurse was saying. 'You can get back to your friends.'

'Couldn't you keep me here a little longer?' he said, joking with her. 'The food's so nice and the nurses so pretty!'

She smiled.

'Couldn't do it if I wanted to!' she said. 'Need your bed for someone else, won't we?'

Then everything slowed right down. He was speaking at a

normal speed, but to me his words came out of his mouth so very, very slowly.

'Fair enough,' he said. 'I'll be a good boy. Let you have the bed back!'

I heard those words, but I heard others too.

This is impossible to explain properly, but all I can say is that I heard him say unspoken words.

'And I'll be dead in the morning anyway.'

They came to me clearly, from across the ward. The nurse kept on teasing him, he joked back, and everything else was perfectly mundane.

I panicked.

'I'll be dead in the morning, anyway.'

I ran from the ward.

I don't think anyone saw me go, but as I got to the doors, I saw Sister Maddox turning into the corridor, coming my way.

Without thinking, I ducked through the nearest door. Shutting it behind me I found myself in the darkness of a linen room. There was one at the end of each ward, full of clean sheets and other bedding.

I crouched in the darkness, wondering if Maddox had seen me, but though footsteps passed outside, the door did not open.

My head was spinning. The feeling of detachment had gone, I was back in my body. I knew that from the way my heart was pounding inside my chest. For a long time, I leant against a stack of blankets and shivered, trying to blot out the words the man *hadn't* spoken.

It was no good. They ran round and round in my mind, though I boxed my ears with my fists, and shook my head from side to side.

Then I thought I heard something.

Something in the linen room with me.

I stood up, and fumbling for where I knew the light switch to be, turned on the small lamp in the ceiling.

'Turn it off,' said a voice.

It came from the far side of the room, on the other side of the shelves of sheets in the centre.

I froze, too scared to do anything.

'Turn it off,' said the voice, again, plaintively. 'It hurts my eyes.'

I did as I was told, and turned if off. Then I realised how rash I was to turn the light off in a small storeroom with an unknown man in there with me.

For I could tell it was a man's voice, though it was small and feeble.

'Who's there?' I asked.

There, was no answer.

'I'm not afraid,' I said. That seems a stupid thing to say, but it's all I could manage.

'Who are you?' I said. 'I'm not afraid.'

'I am,' said the man, 'I am.'

nwittingly, I had said perhaps the one thing that got him to talk.

'What are you afraid of?' I asked.

'Everything,' he said, but there was such feeling behind that single word it made me shiver.

I wondered what I should do. I wanted to run out of the room, but I had always wanted to be a nurse, and if I ran from this chance to help someone, I would have failed.

'Are you sure you wouldn't like the light on?' I asked.

'No!' he said. 'It hurts my eyes. It's better in the dark.'

It was obvious he was a patient.

'Why does it hurt your eyes?' I asked, but that brought no response. I thought about what to say. There was something obvious at least.

'What's your name?'

He answered so quietly I couldn't hear what he said.

'Sorry?'

'Evans,' he said. He paused.

'David Evans.'

I knew he was a soldier, then, from the way he gave his surname first. The name was familiar, but I couldn't place it.

'What are you doing in here, David?' I asked.

'I come here,' he said. 'Get away from the light, the people. That man.'

Now I recognised his Welsh accent.

'No one knows,' he continued. 'Too busy to care, even if they notice. As long as I'm back before bedtime.'

'Why don't you like the light?' I asked again. I was going round in circles, but I couldn't think what else to say.

'It hurts. My eyes hurt. Flashes in the dark, all the time. It hurts my eyes. And now I'm here, and they still want to shine lights into my eyes, see? It hurts, so I come here.'

'Who shines lights into your eyes?' I asked.

'That man,' he said. 'That doctor. Says he wants to look into my eyes, but it hurts, it hurts.'

With a lurching feeling I realised he might be talking about Father. Then it came to me. I knew why his name was familiar.

Evans. He was the shell-shocked patient I'd seen on that very first day with Sister Cave. He was one of the soldiers my father had been doing his tests on.

'They shine it in my eyes,' he said. 'And they stick things to my head.'

'What things?'

'Wires,' he said, in a small voice. 'They stick wires to my head and put electrics through it.'

That was what he said. Electrics.

'Why?' I said, though I knew I was asking the wrong person.

'To make me better, they say, but it hurts, and everything goes weird.'

'Weird? What do you mean?'

I heard noises in the corridor outside. Voices calling and footsteps. Running footsteps. But they went past the door to the linen room.

'What do you mean?' I asked again.

There was silence for a while. I decided to move closer to Evans, even though in the dark I couldn't see him. My legs were starting to cramp, anyway. I stretched, and eased my way round the side of the stacks of blankets.

'What are you doing?' came Evans's voice.

'Just coming closer,' I said. 'I can't hear you properly. Tell me about what happens. When they put the wires on your head.'

'It hurts,' he said, 'and it makes something strange happen. I feel like it's all happened before.'

'What? What's happened before?'

'Everything. The room, them, the wires, the pain. Like it's all happened before, and I'm going through it all over again. Living it again. Do you know what I mean?'

'Yes,' I said, 'I think I do.'

Suddenly there was more commotion outside, coming from the ward.

I felt torn, but I was supposed to be on duty on the ward. I had to see what was going on.

'Stay there, David,' I said to him. 'Don't go anywhere.'

I opened the door and edged out. Everything was happening on the ward. A couple of young doctors rushed past me into the ward and ran to one of the beds.

With a shock I realised that it was the bed of the man with the shrapnel wounds.

Of course it was him. I remember thinking very clearly, that of course it was him. I was disgusted with myself for even wondering who might be in trouble. I ought to have known better than to doubt myself. He said he'd be dead by the morning.

Nurses crowded round, but as the doctors pushed through I

saw there was a pool of blood already collecting on the floor, dripping from the bed.

He was already gone.

I was aware of people around me.

'There you are!' said a voice.

I spun round, but the voice was not directed at me.

Evans stood in the open doorway of the linen room. An orderly, who had been watching the scene in the ward along with me, had spotted him.

'Come on then,' he said, leading Evans away. I could see now that he was a tall, strong young man, at least in body. He looked back at me imploringly, as if I were to blame for his capture.

'Complete case, that one,' said a nurse next to me. 'Shell-shock. Hasn't spoken a word of sensible English since he got here.'

I must have looked puzzled.

'Honestly,' she said. 'Only talks in gibberish. Not a word anyone can understand.'

But that can't be right, one way or another. For although Evans was a frightened, hurt and timid man, I had understood every word he said.

15

I seem to have got away with not being on the ward when I should have been. In the confusion, no one spotted that I wasn't there. I couldn't have done anything to help. I couldn't. Just because I knew it was going to happen doesn't mean I could have stopped it.

I didn't know when he would die, or how. Just that he would.

I feel betrayed now.

Betrayed by my own emotions.

There's a word for what I have been feeling.

Premonitions. Each one has been more clear, more categorical than the last, and they refuse to be ignored.

Although I had not foreseen anyone's death for a long time, there had been no deaths on the ward since I joined. Until yesterday, and the man with shrapnel wounds.

It's not that surprising.

Most men leave the hospital alive, but that's not always much to do with us. Of course, it's a good hospital, and we do our best to see the patients get the help they need, but that's not what I mean. A doctor told me the other day that the truth of the matter is different. He was an older doctor and I didn't like him very much. I think he was trying to scare me. But what he said made awful sense.

He said that if a soldier gets hurt at the front, and if they manage to survive being pulled off the battlefield, and the journey back to the base hospital, and the ship home, then they're probably going to survive, anyway. If they're badly hurt, they'll be dead before they get six miles from the front.

So we don't actually see many deaths, and I am glad of that. But it allows you to think that maybe things aren't as bad as they must really be.

Then yesterday came my clearest premonition. I heard a man tell me he was going to die, and minutes later, he was dead.

There seems no logic to it. It is beyond belief and were it not for the fact that it is happening to me I would not believe it myself. Why do I only see deaths, and not good things? Why do I not see everyone's deaths? As I walk past people in the street, why am I not witnessing all their endings?

A thought strikes me. What if I see something about someone I love, someone in my family? What if I see something about myself?

And if I really can see the future, then what does it mean? Is there any sense in our lives if everything is already out there, just waiting to happen?

For if that were so then life would be a horrible monster indeed, with no chance of escape from fate, from destiny.

It would be like reading a book you know very well, but reading it backwards, from the final chapter, down to chapter one, so that the end is already known to you.

*T*om's letter.

I only remembered it last night as I sat in bed thinking about everything that had happened. I had been late getting home, and Mother fussed over me.

'How are you getting on?' she asked. 'At the hospital?'

I forced a smile.

'Fine,' I said.

Father wasn't home yet, so she can't have known what had happened on the ward. But he wouldn't mention it anyway. Why should he mention a patient dying? It was only to me that it had a terrible significance.

'Just fine?' she said. 'Sasha?'

No. I was not fine. I wanted to shout at her, shake her with words if not with force, and tell her she had to *believe* what was happening to me. It would be the only way she could help me. I stared into the fire, struggling with my feelings, trying to think what was best to say. But I knew.

'Yes, Mother,' I said. 'Everything's fine.'

I even smiled, as I left the room to go up to bed, and she smiled back.

'All right, dear. Sleep well.'

She knows things aren't right with me, but I'm not going to

talk to her about it again. She didn't believe me when I tried before. I wonder when she lost the desire to have a life. I know she cares. I know she loves me. But not enough to cross Father. Not enough to be on my side when it really matters.

I will never let myself become like that, let my spirit be crushed as I see has happened to her . . .

And yet I long for her to make everything all right again, as if I am still her little girl. I long to be a child again, to be naïve, and I long not to know the things I do.

Then I saw Tom's letter, poking out of the pocket of my dress and realised I had forgotten about it.

It's a long letter, about life as a medical student. He says the feeling that we are at war is no different in Manchester; people there are just the same. He stays in a lot, in his digs, when he isn't studying, because he's got into too many arguments about not going to fight.

He thinks the chances of completing his training are small, and that everyone around the college thinks conscription is on its way. He's already had to comply with Compulsory Registration.

> *Now there's this new scheme going on. Have you read about it? They're trying to get all men to say they'll fight if called upon, but they've said they won't ask a married man to fight until the supply of single ones has run out. So there's plenty of married men signing up, looking as though they're doing their bit, but thinking they won't ever have to. And then, of course, when they are needed, they'll get no support from the friends and family of the poor single men who are already dying in France. It's a clever ruse by the government, but quite dishonest.*

That's what Tom says in his letter. He sounds very political, and I don't understand it all. If Father saw what he'd written, I don't think he'd ever let him back in the house.

How can all the people I love so much have such different views on things? But then there are so many contradictions. I love Father but I think the way he runs our house is old-fashioned and cruel. And the way he treats Mother. If he had his way, I'd be married to some rich idiot, and never do what I want to do. But I still love him, and so does Mother, I suppose. And Tom and Father may have different views, but they both want to help people. And me, I feel so alone, but I want to help people too.

In fact, there's someone I badly want to help right now, and who can maybe help me, too.

It wasn't hard to find Evans, even though the one place he never seems to be is in his bed. I'm glad of that, in a way, because the ward for patients like him is not a pleasant place. It's on the top floor of the hospital and even on the floor below you can hear the cries and shouts of the men.

You can dress a wound, put iodine on it, give morphia for the pain, amputate a gangrenous limb. But what can you do for the mind, when it is damaged? I am not sure I know what Father is doing with his colleagues, but I admire them for even trying to help. I wouldn't know where to begin.

But I did know where I would find Evans. He has the run of the hospital it seems. He's less trouble than many of the patients on his ward: some are violent and noisy; or need their sheets changing often; or need hand-feeding. Evans is docile so they don't always bother trying to find him. He comes back when the ward is dark anyway. And on other floors of the hospital everyone's too busy with their own patients.

I didn't know which linen room he'd be in but it wasn't the one he'd been in before. I took the chance when everything was quiet to hunt through the other wards. If anyone stopped me, I would just say I was fetching more blankets.

As soon as I put my head round the door of the fourth

storeroom I'd tried, I knew he was there. I went inside and closed the door.

'I won't turn the light on,' I said.

'Who is it?' came his voice.

'Alexandra; we spoke the other day. Do you remember?'

There was no reply.

'Yes,' he said eventually, his voice dull.

'There's nothing to be—'

'What happened to him?' he asked, interrupting me. 'Did he die?'

'Yes,' I said, trying to sound as calm as possible. 'A wound they didn't know about. Ruptured his lungs.'

We were silent for a while. I wondered how long I could be away for, without being missed.

'May I come closer?' I asked.

I was apprehensive. I was scared, and not because I was afraid of him. He wouldn't harm me, I knew that. No, I was afraid of myself, of what I might feel about him, for although it sounds silly, I feel sorry for Evans, I want him to be all right. I like him.

I moved close to him in the dark, feeling my way round the room.

'May I ask you something?' I said. I felt my knee touch him, and drew back. 'It's about what you told me, about when they put electricity into you.'

'Oh,' he said, in a voice of such unhappiness that I wanted to cry there and then.

'What does it do to you? Would you tell me again?'

There was silence.

'No,' he said.

Then the door opened, and the light came on.

Evans tried to scramble away, knocking over a pile of blankets as he did so.

'Who's there?'

A nurse stepped into view and jumped when she saw us.

'What on earth . . . ?' she began.

I recognised her as the girl who'd shown me around on my first day.

'I was just looking for Evans . . .' I said. 'I was trying . . .'

'I don't want to know what you were doing in here. With him,' she said. Evans tried to make for the door, but she stood in his way. He stopped and waited, squinting against the light.

'No,' I said. 'I was just trying to find him.'

The nurse put her head on one side.

'Is that what you call it? Well, you've found him now. For heaven's sake.'

She turned to Evans.

'You go back to your ward and stay there for once.'

Without a word, he slunk out of the door.

'And you . . .' she said, turning back to me. 'If Sister found you in here with a man, you'd be out of here and never let back. What were you thinking of?'

'Please,' I said, 'please believe me. I wanted to talk to him, that's all. About what they're doing to him.'

She sighed.

'Any other girl in this hospital I might not believe. But you. I don't think you even know why what you've done is so wrong.'

'I only want to know what they're doing to him. He says it hurts.'

She looked surprised now.

'He doesn't say anything that isn't nonsense.'

'He makes sense to me,' I said. 'He says when they put the

wires to his head, he sees things as if they've already happened.'

'He says what?'

Her voice had softened.

'Yes,' I said, encouraged. 'Why do you think that is? What are they trying to do?'

'They're trying to make him better,' she said.

'But it hurts him. Why are they doing it?'

'He's your father, why don't you ask him?'

'Please,' I said. 'You don't understand. I need to know. Things have been happening to me, that I . . .'

'What things?' she asked.

I hesitated, but couldn't help myself.

'I see things,' I said. 'I see things before they happen.'

She took a step backwards, and flicked off the light, without warning.

'I think you'd better get back to work,' she said, her voice sharp and thin. 'Don't you?'

12

*W*hen I got home there was all sorts of pandemonium in the house. I could hear Mother in the kitchen, her voice high and loud, almost wailing at Father.

They stopped talking the moment I came in.

'What's wrong?' I asked.

Mother hurried past me, her hand to her mouth.

I saw a letter on the table.

'What is it?' I said, turning to Father.

He put up his hand.

'Edgar's been wounded. Don't worry,' he added, quickly. 'He's fine.'

'Father?'

'Yes, he's fine. He couldn't write that if he wasn't, could he?'

'What happened?' I asked.

'Not sure, exactly,' he said, shaking his head. 'But it's just a scratch. He spent a few days in hospital in Boulogne, in the middle of November. He's back with his battalion now. Fighting fit!'

'But what happened?'

'That's enough, Alexandra! Do you not realise you upset your mother with all your questions?'

That seemed unfair. Mother was already upset before I got

home, and had already left the room. But I knew not to say anything more, not while Father was in that kind of mood.

I looked at the letter. Edgar's letter from France, lying on the kitchen table. I wanted to read it, but Father picked it up and left the room.

I followed him and as he went into his study, I made my way upstairs, pausing just long enough to see him put the letter in the drawer of his writing desk. Then I found Molly and asked her to bring me something to eat in my room. I went up to bed.

*M*olly brought me soup and some bread. I ate it slowly, thoughtfully, thinking things through.

My eyes fell on Miss Garrett's book. I hadn't looked at it for ages. I picked it up and flicked through it. Cassandra. Her name leapt out at me from page after page. Daughter of King Priam of Troy. She was given the gift of prophecy by Apollo, but because she refused to sleep with him in return, he cursed her gift, making sure that no one would ever believe her. She ended her life telling of the doom of Troy, but still no one believed her. It didn't matter in the end, because everything she saw happened anyway, including her own death. Taken captive by Agamemnon, spirited away from Troy to Argos, she was slain by Agamemnon's jealous wife.

Perhaps she went crazy waiting for someone finally to believe her, to take notice of her, to let her help.

And did she gaze out on a view of the sea, like I do? Maybe she did, dreading the conflict that was to come across the water. Did she feel alone, as I do? Maybe she looked at her reflection as I have done, trying to see what was different about her, trying to understand her gift?

A gift, or a curse? I knew which I thought it was. The book

trembled in my hand. I shut it before my tears ruined something which I'd promised to take good care of.

After Mother and Father had gone to bed I went back down to the study. On Father's desk is a green-shaded reading lamp. I put the lamp on and began to open the small drawers in the back of the desk.

Edgar's letter was easy to find, I could smell it almost before I saw it. It smelt of cold air, of damp, of earth, of smoke. It was only a few weeks old and yet looked as though it had seen more history than most of us will see in our whole lives.

I have the letter in front of me now.

At the top, in Edgar's handwriting, it says: *No. 14 Stationary Hospital, Boulogne. 13 November.*

It's taken over three weeks for the letter to get here. It's a very short letter, really. I suppose he must have been exhausted while he was in hospital, and unable to write much.

> *Dear Family,*
> *I am well, but I must tell you I have received a small*
> *injury which has put me in hospital. Don't worry, though,*
> *it is nothing serious. A shell exploded near our dug-out,*
> *and I took a small piece in my chest. I will be back in*
> *action, soon.*
>
> *I send you my best wishes,*
> *Your Edgar.*

I thought I might feel something from the letter, that I might see something while holding it, but nothing happened. And I had had no inkling of Edgar's injury, though it happened weeks ago. I had not suspected a thing. So this curse I have cannot even be relied upon to be consistent. To actually be of some use.

But I wonder why the letter smells of the battlefield, when it was written from hospital. Maybe I can sense something of Edgar from it, after all.

*I*t is Monday evening.

The weekend was a miserable affair. Mother was quiet. She was worrying about Edgar, I knew, and the one time she did speak it was of him.

'I wonder where Edgar will be for Christmas,' she said.

Not such a bad thing to say, but it was enough to irritate Father, for some reason. He raised his voice, told her to stop fretting about Edgar all the time. Then he went out.

That was Saturday morning, and as soon as he had gone, I took the chance to replace Edgar's letter in Father's desk before it was missed. That would only cause more trouble.

I tried to comfort Mother not by talking but by doing. I took her out shopping but she stared at things in a listless way, and would barely speak to the shop assistants.

In Needham's Mother stopped by the glove counter.

Hoping to catch her interest, I asked her if she wanted new gloves for the winter.

She didn't answer, but simply stared at the counter.

'Mother?' I tried again. 'Did you want something?'

Still she gazed down, saying nothing. I could see an assistant dithering, wondering whether to come over or not.

'Mother?'

91

'I wonder if Edgar's hands are warm.'

I looked at the assistant and smiled, but shook my head to keep her away.

'I'm sure he's fine,' I said.

'But it must be cold, and wet.'

'He'll be all right, Mother. Remember how smart he looked in his uniform? He'll have everything he needs.'

'Do you think so, Sasha?'

Now at least she stopped looking at the gloves and looked at me, but the weight of the pain in her eyes was enough to break my heart.

'Yes,' I whispered. 'I'm sure of it. Come away now. Let's go to Hannington's, see if they have your material.'

I nearly had to pull her out of the shop, but at last we were outside. It was raining by then and we gave up. To be honest, I was relieved that the shopping trip was over.

We came home and I got changed for a late afternoon shift.

It was bitter, wretched weather as I made my way up to Seven Dials and crossed over towards the hospital.

The rain began to lash down again as the hospital came in sight, so I ran for the entrance.

As I passed through the doors I felt better immediately. Better, almost happier in a way, despite everything that has happened here. I was glad of the warmth of the place, and of the noise and the brightness. For a second I stopped and marvelled at the commotion, people coming and going, nurses and orderlies going about their work, and I realised that I had come to like the place, in quite a short time.

'Fox,' smiled one of the nurses as she passed, and nodded to me.

I smiled back and got to work.

It was a quiet shift, but there were two pieces of interesting news.

First of all was Sister Maddox. I could tell something was different on the ward as soon as I arrived, but it took me a while to learn what.

'Have you heard?' the nurses said to me. 'About Maddox.'

'She's gone!'

'She's gone to France.'

My face must have shown my surprise.

'I know,' someone said. 'We were as surprised as you are! Apparently, she felt she wasn't doing enough here. She got herself sent to France, to a hospital in Rouen.'

Maddox had seemed such a hard, uncaring woman. Maybe that's not such an uncommon thing in the medical profession, but perhaps we were wrong about her. She didn't tell anyone she was going, and left without a word to any of her staff. She hasn't been replaced, at least not yet, but that's not unusual. More and more nurses are making their way out to France to the big hospitals, in Paris, in Rouen, where Maddox has gone, or Boulogne, where Edgar was when he was injured. They have to volunteer, and then wait to be called up. I know Father's responsible for passing the applications of nurses from our hospital.

I've overheard him talk about things in France. I know what he'd say: 'always watching, always prying.' But that's how I learn, by watching.

The existing French hospitals were soon overwhelmed at the start of the war, and many other buildings, like hotels and warehouses, have been put to use as makeshift hospitals. And all these hospitals need nurses, especially ones as experienced as Sister Maddox. But I still find it hard to imagine her wanting to go to France.

The other thing that I learnt was even more of a shock.

On my way home after my shift, I saw a nurse I knew walking the same way as me, though on the other side of the road. We must have the same shift patterns, because I keep bumping into her. It was the nurse who had found me in the linen room with Evans.

I ducked my head and tried to pretend I hadn't seen her, but she had seen me. I tried to hurry, but she skipped across the road to walk beside me.

'Wait!' she said. 'I want to tell you something. It's about your friend. Evans. The Welshman?'

'Leave me alone,' I said, unhappily, and kept on walking.

'No,' she said. 'No . . . listen. I thought you might like to know. He's making sense again. I mean, he's getting better.'

I slowed down, and looked sideways at her, trying to judge if she were teasing or not.

'Whatever it was you did, it worked. All the nurses are talking about it, about how you made him better.'

I stopped.

'How do they know?' I asked. 'Who told them?'

The girl blushed and I had my answer.

'Don't worry,' she said, hurriedly. 'It's just nurses' gossip. Your father . . . I mean, the doctors won't take any notice of that, they'll think it was what they did to him that worked.'

'Maybe it was,' I said.

She shrugged.

'Anyway,' she said, 'I just thought you'd like to know.'

'Thank you,' I said, and I meant it.

Last night I dreamed about the raven again.

It was a vivid dream, so lifelike, that when I woke in the middle of the night, my heart racing, it seemed real.

I was flying. Flying high above a darkening landscape, and without any reason I knew I was above the plains outside the city of Troy. Was I seeing what Cassandra had seen?

The sun was setting. In truth, I knew that for the people on the ground far below me the sun had already set, but looking down from on high, I could still see the last cusp of the red sun slipping beneath the far horizon. It flickered once more like the embers of coal in a fire, then went out. Night came and wrapped the earth in its dusky wings. Darkness flooded across the landscape from the west, but I somehow could see clearly.

I whirled and soared like a bird of prey, and some distance away I could see the walls of the great city, the top of which bristled with feather-laden spear tips. But my attention was drawn to the fields beneath me, from where I felt a terrible pull of death, as if the departing souls of the slaughtered men were trying to take me with them.

I resisted.

I resisted and tried to pull up into the sky and soar again, but

I could not. I began to plummet towards the earth as I realised it was impossible that I should be flying anyway.

The ground hurtled toward me, but somehow with infinite slowness, so that I had time to gaze at the horrors that unfolded there. All around was carnage, and bloodied bodies. Broken chariots and splintered shields were strewn across the plains as if cast there by a god's hand. Here and there a few men still wearily tried to put an end to each other, but this was a battle that was already dead itself.

I landed, and in mild surprise saw that I had survived the fall, and landed on my feet, my legs merely jarred by the impact.

It was then that I saw the raven. It was a huge bird, and at first I could only marvel at its beauty. The blackness of its feathers was perfect; a glistening, oily blackness set off by the charcoal grey of its beak. It fixed an eye on me and put its head on one side, and only then did I see what it was standing on, what it had been feeding on.

I thought I was going to be sick, but I could not look away, and then the bird spoke to me.

It spoke with the voice of the dead upon which it was feeding.

'You!' it said. 'You alone saw the horror of war, and wept when we did not believe you.'

I woke.

*T*homas has come home.

It's so wonderful, that I had to struggle not to cry when he walked through the front door. I threw my arms around him to hide the tears in my eyes.

He laughed, and pushed me away.

'Sasha!' he cried, and everyone laughed, even Father, though there was nothing really to laugh at.

'You've grown,' Mother declared.

Tom groaned.

'Don't be silly,' Father said. 'He hasn't grown. You shrank him in your memory.'

I think Father might be right about that, but Mother was right too. There was something different about Tom. I don't think he was any taller, but he was older. He had aged by more than the few months he'd been away.

Father stepped forward. I wondered what he was doing, but then he put out his hand. Tom looked at it for a moment and then shook it.

It was the first time that they've ever done this and I immediately knew what it meant. Father considers Thomas to be a man, and as I watched I smiled inside for what I hope it means.

*T*om and I have been catching up today, swapping stories of hospital life, he as a medical student and me as a voluntary nurse.

We chatted as we helped Mother make Christmas pudding, rather late this year. This is one job she likes to do herself, and not leave to Cook. She bustled around the kitchen, getting Molly to fetch ingredients for her as she needed them. She was busy, she seemed happy, and I saw that she smiled, listening to us talk, as she stirred in a bottle of brown ale and a bottle of stout.

Father came home later and we had supper. It was quiet at first, and I felt nervous for some reason.

Father looked at Tom, a forkful of food in one hand.

'So how are your studies, Tom?'

Tom's face lit up.

'Everything's going well,' he said. 'There's only a few of us really, because lots of boys deferred entry to go to—'

He stopped.

Father nodded.

'Go on,' Mother said. 'Tell us about Manchester.'

Tom shrugged.

'It's well enough,' he said. 'It's not as nice as Brighton, but the people are friendly. Well, most of them.'

I could tell he was thinking of the white feathers he's been given. I knew more about that than Mother or Father because Tom knows it upsets them, though in different ways.

Tom talked for a bit, and we ate, and then Father put his knife and fork down and looked at Tom.

'I'm sure that any son of mine could make a fine doctor,' he said. 'But I think you may not have the chance to find out for a while.'

Tom's head dropped.

Father was talking about conscription. It seems more likely than ever that a bill will be passed soon.

'If we start now we can get you a commission in the Medical Corps, and then you can do your bit as well as do what you feel is right.'

Father was trying to compromise between what he thinks Tom should do and what Tom wants to do, and I was amazed that he said it, because Father is not a man who usually compromises on anything.

But Tom let his head sink a little further, and would eat no more supper.

I saw Evans today, and it seems to be true. He seems to be better. I was wheeling a trolley between wards when I heard someone behind me.

'How are you, today, Nurse?' he asked, as if he made small talk like this every day of his life.

I smiled.

'Fine . . .' I stuttered out, eventually. 'Fine.'

'That's good,' he said. He stood smiling at me, waiting for me to speak.

'And how are you?' was all I could manage, but as I spoke I saw from the corner of my eye that three nurses on the other side of the corridor were watching us with interest.

I started to wheel forward again, but Evans was talking to me now.

'Very well,' he said. 'Thank you, Nurse. Very well.'

'You look much better, I must say,' I said.

I was still aware that we were being watched and I was afraid.

'Yes, yes,' he said. 'Wonderful what the doctors have done for me, it is.'

I thought about what he had said before, about the tests, about the lights and being hurt.

'Everything's right now, is it? The tests, before . . . ? They didn't . . . ?'

'Oh no,' he said quickly, smiling.

I started to feel uneasy.

'But what you said,' I persisted, 'about feeling as though you had already seen things once before. What about that?'

He stopped smiling and stood up straight, stiff. For the first time I could actually imagine that he could be a soldier.

'I don't know what you're talking about,' he said, and turned on his heels.

I looked at the nurses who had been watching and they pretended to be busy.

I wheeled my trolley on to the ward.

I feel let down. Of course it's good that Evans is better – and I feel guilty for even thinking this – but when everyone thought he was crazy, I thought I had found one person who I could confide in. And now he's better he denies we ever spoke of such things.

If I only took heart from a discussion with a man while he was mad, what does that say about me?

Tom and I went Christmas shopping today. It didn't feel quite right, because Edgar won't be home this year. Nonetheless, we must try to make Christmas as normal as possible, and buy each other some small token or other, and do everything else you do.

After a fruitless and tiring morning we decided that parents are impossible to buy presents for, and took a short cut down one of the twitters that runs off Middle Street, to shelter in a small café in the Lanes, even though it's an area of town Father doesn't like us to visit.

We ordered buttered toast and tea and, hidden away in a corner by the window, I felt safer and happier than I had for a long time. I had been occupied at the hospital, but with Tom, I knew I felt truly safe. But I felt tired too, and said so to Tom.

'Why?' he asked.

'There's been so much going on,' I said.

'At the hospital?' he asked.

'Yes,' I said. I stopped.

'There must be a lot to learn. Some of it must be pretty horrible, too.'

I nodded, and sipped my tea.

I looked out of the window at the narrow twisting passages

of the Lanes. I could see a small slit of sky above the rooftops. It seemed likely to rain again soon.

'Are you all right?' Tom asked.

'Yes,' I said.

'But are you enjoying it?'

'I don't know,' I said. 'I haven't thought about it like that. But yes, I suppose I am.'

He stretched a hand across the table to mine.

'Then what's wrong?'

I didn't answer.

'What's wrong, Sasha? I can tell something's getting to you. You're different from when I went away. Is Father being mean?'

I shook my head.

'No more than usual.' I smiled. 'In fact, he's been quite generous at times.'

'So what is it?'

I looked at my brother, and then looked away. He was so kind to me, he always had been, and he was open-minded and clever. If there was one person I could talk to, it was him.

I squeezed his hand briefly, then pushed it away.

'I'm fine,' I said. 'Do you want some more tea?'

I couldn't do it.

He was the one person who might believe me, but if he, of all people, reacted the way everyone else had, it would hurt more than I could bear.

When we got home, we found Mother and Father in the drawing room. They had a visitor. Miss Garrett.

Mother forced a smile as we came in.

'Miss Garrett stopped by to see you,' she said, but Father cut across her.

'To have a talk about your studying,' he said. I looked from Mother to Miss Garrett, who seemed uncomfortable.

'Sit down, Alexandra,' Father said. 'Tom?'

Tom shuffled awkwardly in the doorway, then backed out, nodding to Miss Garrett and closing the door behind him.

'Mother?' I said, and felt very small.

Mother looked at her hands and then at Father.

'We understand that your work has been poor recently,' Father said.

'I only said . . .' Miss Garrett began, but Father interrupted.

'We are very disappointed.'

It all started to come out then.

'Alexandra, you're an intelligent girl,' Mother said.

'But you've been so distracted lately,' Miss Garrett said.

I couldn't think what to say, I knew it was true.

'Miss Garrett says you borrowed a book from her,' Father said. 'Will you please go and get it.'

I hesitated, wondering what all this was about.

'Sasha. Please.' Mother said.

She looked so upset I wanted to shake her, but I went and got the book. Father took it from me and glanced through it.

'Why did you want this book when you haven't been paying attention?'

I frowned.

'I wanted to read the stories,' I said. 'I thought I'd better make an effort to catch up.'

It wasn't strictly true, but it was the best I could manage.

'The Trojan Wars?' Father said. 'Achilles? Ajax? Helen and Paris?'

'Your recollection of the classics is admirable,' said Miss Garrett, with false jollity. She misread Father's tone entirely.

'And Cassandra, too?' he said, his voice loud. 'Is that it?'

I could see what he thought, but I didn't know what I could say. As usual his mind was made up.

I shrugged.

There was silence for a long time.

63

*M*iss Garrett left shortly after that, making some embarrassed excuse and hurrying out into the evening with Mother
fretting at her heels, pushing the copy of *Greek Myths* back into
her hands as she went.

I really don't think she meant to get me into such trouble.
She's not a strict tutor, and she means well. I think she was
probably genuinely worried about me.

Mother dithered in the doorway, but Father wouldn't let her
back in, telling her to find Cook and that he wanted his dinner
soon. She saw the look on his face and went off to the kitchen
without speaking further.

'Father,' I said. 'I haven't done anything wrong.'

'Be quiet!' he shouted.

I sat down and felt myself shaking.

'Why do my children insist on making a fool of me?' he said,
but I knew it was not a question I should reply to.

'What did you talk about?' he snapped.

'I . . . Do you mean, with Miss Garrett?' I asked.

'No, I do not and you know I do not!'

I didn't understand, I really didn't, and Father had to spell it
out, though I could see he didn't want to.

'The patient,' he seethed. 'The Welshman.'

'Father,' I said, pleading, 'nothing. I said nothing. He talked to me, I asked him how he was. That was all!'

'It was not all.'

'I swear it,' I said.

'You talked about his treatment. About me! Admit it!'

'No, Father, no,' I said, tears running down my face.

'You talked about the tests and the electrical stimulations. About the *déjà vu* he claimed to experience. Well, it's all nonsense.'

I said nothing. It was clear someone had told Father and there was no point denying it anymore.

'You have been living a fantasy life, Alexandra; a fantasy. You have been idolising the neurasthenic patients like Evans, and filling your head with wild myths from books!'

He paused then, as if I were supposed to say something, but I couldn't. There was nothing I could say.

'You are nearly a woman, now, Alexandra. Did you ever stop to think what effect your childish imaginings would have on someone who'd lost a relative? Pretending you knew it was going to happen? How distasteful! How disrespectful! To make a game from their suffering!'

'No, Father!' I cried. 'That's not fair. It's not true. I haven't hurt anyone.'

'Maybe not,' he said. 'But I'm not going to give you the chance. You are not to go back to the hospital.'

'Father . . . ?'

'You heard me. I forbid you to continue nursing. That's over now. You will go back to studying properly and conduct yourself in a manner more fitting to a young lady of your class. And that is all.'

He left the room, and a few moments later, I heard him leave the house, heedless that dinner was on the way.

I do not think he will change his mind.

62

A generation of men is like the leaves on the trees. When the winter winds blow, the leaves are scattered to the ground, but with spring, a new generation of men bursts into bud, to replace those that went before. But this is a harsh winter, the like of which has never been seen before.

I think of the words from my dream, croaked to me by that evil bird on the battlefield.

> *'You saw the horrors of war, and wept when we did not believe you.'*

I don't fully understand what it is that I have done, in Father's eyes. I don't understand what is so terrible, but I have been punished, anyway. Not just with words, but with deeds too. I am not to be allowed to continue nursing.

And all for something I did not wish for. A power which has been given to me, to see endings, but to be unable to prevent them, or even to make others believe what I have seen. In idle fantasy you might think that to see the future would be a wonderful gift, but it's not.

It's nothing but a curse.

*I*t's nearly Christmas.

I have not been to the hospital, nor anywhere near it. I have seen no more visions of the future, and yet still I feel fate swirling around me like leaves caught in those tiny whirlwinds that eddy in the autumn streets.

Today, for example, there was another coincidence. I was walking home from Miss Garrett's in Preston Park, and was surprised when a soldier coming up the hill stopped in front of me.

'Hello, Nurse,' he said. 'And goodbye, I suppose.'

It was David Evans. I think it was the uniform that stopped me from recognising him immediately.

I struggled for words. I knew that it was perhaps because of what he'd said that I'd lost my position, but I didn't want to talk about that. It wasn't his fault, he probably didn't even remember anything about it now.

'Are you leaving?' I asked, though it was obvious. He had a kit bag on his back and was heading for the station.

'I am, indeed,' he said, smiling, as if it were the most natural thing in the world. 'Got to get back to my mates. That's important. Stick together, we do. That's the only way.'

110

I nodded.

'Yes,' I said, 'yes. Don't you have family to see first?'

'No family, no,' he said. 'The boys, the sergeant-major. That's my family. See?'

I nodded again.

'Well, better be along, got to get the train to Southampton. Catch a boat, you know!'

I smiled.

'One last thing,' he said. 'May I give you a kiss?'

I took a step backwards, but I could see he meant no harm.

'If I tell the boys I kissed a girl as beautiful as you,' he said, laughing, 'they'll be green fit to burst!'

I laughed too.

'Very well,' I said. 'Are all Welshmen as charming as you?'

'Not quite,' he said, winking.

He leant down and kissed me quickly on the cheek, like an uncle.

As he straightened up again I noticed he was looking at me thoughtfully. At my eyes.

'What is it?' I asked.

'Nothing,' he said, casually, 'nothing. I just . . . Well, anyway, I must be going now. Goodbye.'

He slung his kit bag over his shoulder, and set off to the station once more.

I felt a little glow of satisfaction inside, as he went – though I never thought that my first kiss would come from a Welsh soldier.

I was puzzled. He seemed to have made such a complete recovery from the wrecked shell of a man he had been when I

111

first saw him. I knew that didn't often happen with shell-shock, and I spent the rest of the day wondering what had made him better.

Christmas has come. It's Friday evening, and tomorrow is Christmas Day.

Earlier this evening, we sat in the drawing room, and all had a glass of sherry, even me. Mother asked me to play some carols on the piano, which I was happy to do for her, though my heart wasn't really in it. I played quite badly but Mother and Father and Tom sang along and thanked me for playing when I finished.

I am angry with Father for stopping me from being a VAD nurse. I am sad that Mother hasn't tried to get him to change his mind, and frustrated that Tom is unable to speak out for me.

His own situation is hard enough, with the tension between Father and him over joining the army. Tom remains adamant that he wants to continue his training until he is forced not to. If he were to try and intercede on my behalf we both know it wouldn't help either of our causes.

We had a Christmas card from Edgar. I don't know how he managed to get time to send it. It's French and very jolly and shows some young ladies on a sleigh, wrapped in furs. *Joyeux Noel* it says in ornate writing across the front.

It had come a few days ago, but Father kept it hidden as a surprise and read it out to us this evening.

Dear Family,

I trust you are all together at home now in Clifton Terrace. I wish I could be with you, too, but you know that I must be here. Nevertheless, I wish you all a Merry Christmas. We're hoping for a bit of a do ourselves, God willing, so don't worry about me. I must go now.

Your Edgar.

Father put it up on the mantelpiece, in pride of place, moving a card from someone else aside to do so.

Mother was delighted.

'You were naughty to keep it from us,' she chided Father, gently.

He smiled, and kissed her on the forehead.

'But it's the best Christmas present we could have had,' I said, and everyone agreed.

Then we had a supper of goose and gravy, and went to bed happy.

I am tired now, it is late, and Christmas is here.

59

The nightmare I was dreading has started.

I don't know what to do.

I don't know.

I woke early, but not with the excitement of Christmas morning. I woke in the grip of fear. And my heart pounding so hard it hurt.

A thought came into my head from nowhere.

The Christmas card. Edgar's Christmas card. I suddenly realised that after Father had produced it and read it to us, he put it straight on the mantelpiece.

I had not touched it.

But I have now.

I went downstairs, took it from the shelf, turned it over and read it myself.

That was hours ago. I don't even remember how I got back upstairs. I must have run here for safety, to my own place.

I don't know what to do.

I have the card in front of me, and cannot stop looking at it, at the writing.

Writing that is now stained with my tears.

I can still see what it says, in Edgar's writing, but it is what I heard when I read it the first time that has told me what I most fear.

The words are there just as they were before, when Father read them. But as I read them I heard Edgar's voice, and he was saying something quite different.

> *'I must go now. I had a bayonet put into my back as I was doing the same to another man. I must go now. I am dead and I must go.'*

I heard it only once, but it was clear enough; the minute I touched the card a shock shot through me.

> *'I am dead and I must go.'*

I have sat for hours, shaking and crying. I am too scared to do anything, to talk to anyone. It is light outside now, I can hear the gulls screeching dimly at the back of my brain, but I cannot move.

I can't even bring myself to get Tom, though I want him to be here more than anything.

I know I'm right, but no one will believe me.

What am I going to do?

There's a knock at the door.

I look to see what time it is. Later than I thought. It's gone nine.

It strikes me dumbly that no one knocks on a door at nine o'clock on Christmas morning.

I know who it is.

I hear Mother going downstairs.

Clutching Edgar's card, I open my door, go down the stairs and reach the top of the landing, just as Mother opens the front door.

I hear one word, spoken quietly, in a tone of terrible respect.
'Telegram.'
That's all.
And then I hear Mother screaming.
She's screaming and screaming.

58

*T*hough the events of Christmas morning are months ago now, I can still see them all as if it has just happened. In some ways I can see things even more clearly now than I could at the time, because then my vision was obscured by shock and pain.

Now there's only pain.

*T*omorrow will be the twenty-fifth of June.

It's six months since we heard that Edgar had been killed. It is five days more than that since the actual moment, but details are still hard to come by.

The telegram was brief, and to the point, and to be honest, it didn't really matter at the time. But now I want to find out more about it. I want to know everything, though we may never know it all.

We had a memorial service for Edgar in early January, but there was no funeral, because there was no body to bury. He was buried somewhere in Belgium, in a military cemetery.

A letter we had later from a friend of his, another captain in his battalion, said he had been killed leading a raiding party into the enemy trenches. He said Edgar had been very brave and the raid had been a big success.

But that's a lie.

Just as I had heard Edgar tell me he was dead, I had seen a horrible tableau of the moment.

The panic. The complete chaos. No one was brave, not Englishman, nor German; there was only horror and fear and utter bestial panic as Edgar's party arrived in the wrong place, as they killed and were killed, and as a couple of lucky men

119

managed to stagger back to their own trench, their only success being alive to report what a disaster the whole thing had been.

But I said nothing of that to anyone.

Mother and Father cling desperately to the idea that their son died a hero's death, as if it makes any difference. Death is death. But if it helps them to think that, then it is well enough, I suppose.

*S*ix months.

The longest of my life. We have been pretending, and pretending, and pretending, all this time. That life could go on, that the war would end soon, that Edgar would come home, that it isn't really happening.

Now we know the truth.

Mother is broken, Father is sullen, and Thomas?

Thomas has gone.

That is almost the saddest thing about Edgar's death.

Something changed in him, that Christmas morning.

He didn't cry, not like Mother and me. Father shouted and cursed, but Tom went silent, immediately.

Now he is in France.

55

*I*t was only a few days after the telegram arrived, maybe not even into the New Year, that Thomas told us he was going to join the army, after all.

Mother took it badly, and begged him not to go, but Father . . .

I had thought he would have been overjoyed, even delighted that he had finally won the argument with Thomas, but he wasn't.

'Very well,' he said, but his voice was toneless. 'You should go. I am proud of you for coming to the right decision. You can make *us* proud and keep the memory of your brother alive.'

I can't believe what Tom did when Father said that.

He hit him.

There and then, he struck him across the chin. Father stumbled back and sank into a chair, but what is even more amazing is what happened next.

Nothing.

I was ready for Father to explode, to beat Tom, throw him out, at the very least curse him. But he did nothing.

He sat in the chair, looking like a tired old man, and rubbed his chin.

Tom glared at us all, then turned on his heel and left. As he went I saw drops of blood from his knuckles stain the carpet in the hall.

5

*T*hat moment, six months ago now, that lives on so vividly with me, was forgotten, or rather ignored by us all.

Tom went back to Manchester after Edgar's memorial, hardly saying another dozen words to any of us.

Not even to me, and I could hardly bear that.

One thing was clear, he intended to join up.

Father made some phone calls, and once again, as with Edgar, he managed to secure a commission in the Royal Army Medical Corps on the strength of Tom's public school background, and his OTC experience there.

Then, without warning, Tom arrived back in Brighton. Father had been trying to make contact with him for days, to let him know about his commission, and was a little annoyed when he just strolled into the kitchen through the back door one day in January.

'I'm leaving,' he said.

We all looked puzzled; he had only just arrived back.

'I'm leaving for France,' he explained.

'I don't understand,' Mother said. 'Father's got you a place in the RAMC, you can't be leaving yet.'

Tom looked from her to Father.

Neither of them said anything, then Tom put his hand out

awkwardly to Father. He left it there for what seemed an age, until finally Father took it and shook it.

'Thank you,' he said.

Mother smiled.

'It'll be fine in the RAMC,' Father said. 'Much safer, but you can still . . . you know. Help.'

Tom stepped back abruptly.

'No,' he said. 'You don't understand. I'm grateful to you for trying, for getting me the place. But I'm not taking it.'

'What?' Father said, his voice pinched with disbelief.

'I'm not taking a commission. I've enlisted with the 20th Fusiliers, in Manchester, the Public Schools Battalion. As a private.'

I saw Mother put her hand to her throat, and the colour drained from her cheeks.

I stood up and grabbed Tom, pleaded with him not to go, but he wouldn't listen to me, to any of us.

I asked him what had changed, why he didn't want to be a doctor any more, and a hundred other things, but he wouldn't talk.

Mother was trying, and failing, not to cry, Father stomped around the kitchen, starting sentences, then stopping them, hot under the collar.

'But Tom,' Mother pleaded, 'you'll be safer in the RAMC, and you want to be a doctor, don't you? Don't you?'

Tom looked at her, miserably, his lip trembling.

'There's no use in it.'

That's all he would say.

53

*H*e left in January. It's June now. Winter ended, spring came and went and now summer is here.

The house is so quiet. Father is working longer hours than ever. Mother speaks of nothing but what is necessary, and I have been left to myself, day in, day out, going crazy.

I have far too much time to think, far too much.

I think about everything that has happened to me, and to my family, and it does me no good at all. I pray like the stupid little girl I am to be young again. For all this not have happened. For Edgar to be alive and for Tom to be happy. I long to be a young girl playing in a summer's garden, but even that desire has bad memories. Then I understand how naïve I am. That past, that happy past, is gone. Long gone. I will never have it back. Now I can see what it is that put distance between me and my family. It goes all the way back to Clare. Mother was scared by it, and has spent all her time since then trying to keep at bay a future she didn't want me to face. Father disbelieved it, and withdrew from me, and Edgar took his lead from Father, as always. Only Tom kept some faith with me, probably just because he was too young to do otherwise than keep loving his little sister.

And that's the feeling I've had all this time. Guilt that I

lost my family because of what I am, and that they lost faith in me.

One day, I tried to talk to Father about becoming a nurse again.

He seemed to listen, but he wouldn't agree. Then I made the mistake of reminding him that Edgar had said I should have the chance to be a nurse, and that I ought to be given the chance again.

It was a mistake to mention Edgar's name.

At the end of May, it was my birthday.

I am eighteen.

In a few days' time it will be Thomas's birthday. On the first of July he will be nineteen. I wonder where he will be. He rarely writes. When he was in Manchester he wrote all the time, but he is silent now. Of course, it is harder for him to write than it was for Edgar. Edgar was an officer and had more privileges. Tom is a private, and all we have had from him are two or three postcards that the army issues. They have a list of banal phrases on them, and Tom just crosses out the ones that don't apply.

Both times he has crossed out all the phrases on the card except the first.

I am quite well.

And he has signed it. That is all we know.

52

*N*ow I know something more, something that I wish I did not know.

I had had no more premonitions since the moment I touched Edgar's Christmas card, but last night the raven came back to me in a dream.

I heard the beat of its wings, drumming louder and louder.

It came right up close to me.

Its wing drifted across in front of my face – so close that I could see the barbs of each feather. The wing swung like a huge black curtain across the stage of a theatre, and lifted to reveal a thousand ravens swinging around the treetops of a blighted wood.

The ravens parted, and I saw a gun.

The gun fired, with a violent bang that shook me awake in an instant.

Just before I was pushed out of the dream, I glimpsed one more thing.

The bullet's target.

Thomas.

It hit him. He's going to die.

51

At last my time has come.

I know it from the foreshadowing of Thomas's death.

I don't know how, but as I lay awake shivering after the dream, I know it hasn't happened, and that maybe it won't for some time. It is definitely something that has yet to be.

I don't know why this is happening to me, or how it does. It feels as if someone is playing games with me, with my life, my destiny. Or with that of my family.

Finally I have the chance to do something with what I have seen.

I know it is no use to talk to my parents about it. They thought I was living with fantasies before. If I tell them I know Tom is going to die, they'll probably think I've gone mad.

I have to live with this curse now, the curse that is to know the future but never to be believed.

The sight came to me before; for Clare, for that soldier, for Edgar's friend, for those patients. For Edgar himself, but it did no good.

What was the use? Edgar was dead, but I had no warning; I only knew a few moments before we found out anyway, from the telegram.

But this time . . .

This time is different – I've been given some time to do something with what I have seen. And even if I am wrong, it makes no difference to what I have decided.

There's a big offensive due to start soon; the papers have been full of it. The British and French armies have been gearing up for something massive for months, or so we are led to believe. If that's true then many men will die, but Tom isn't going to be one of them, because I'm going to stop it.

I've planned it all.

Although Father has kept me from the hospital, on several occasions I have bumped into nurses that I know. We've chatted, and they've told me about the comings and goings. I know lots of young girls have been volunteering to go to France as Red Cross nurses. The hospitals there are desperate for them.

I know where they sail from, and to, and where they go next. The boats leave almost all the time from Folkestone. Dover's too dangerous, so they sail from Folkestone, a bit further down the coast. From there they head to Boulogne, or to Rouen, and unload, among other things, the latest supply of willing voluntary nurses.

And tomorrow, there's going to be one more nurse joining them.

I don't know where Tom's battalion is, but I know they're somewhere in Flanders, and once I'm there, it shouldn't be too hard to find out where.

Then I'm going to bring him home, and stop his death ever having the chance to happen.

If it's true that I lost my family, and that they lost their faith in me, then this is my chance to mend it all. I want to heal the rift between us, make everything all right again. If I save Tom, then maybe they'll understand me at last, and I will get them back.

I will save Tom.

It's my only hope, but I can do it.

I must.

Part Two

50

I have been in France for nearly a week, and this is the first chance I have had to stop and think.

A week, but it feels like a year, so much has happened.

As I was on the ship, I thought vaguely that I would keep a diary of my journey in France, but I see what a ridiculous idea that was. There wouldn't have been time, and one week's experience of the real nature of the war is enough to make me want to forget everything I've seen, not make a permanent record of it.

It's Saturday morning, and I am sitting in the canteen. All around me are the noises of the rest station, and the sound of trains. I can scarcely believe I'm here, in France. Soon, I will be moved to work in No. 13 Stationary Hospital, based in huts up on the cliffs, but I'm being given two weeks' experience in the rest station first. They say it will give me a taste of what I am likely to encounter. I couldn't tell them, of course, that I don't intend staying that long. As soon as I can find out where Tom is, I'll be moving on.

The rest station is part of the railway station, convened from rooms along the platform into a suite for ambulance work. We have a surgery and dispensary, a storeroom, and a staff room. We cook outside on large portable boilers.

The reason the rest station is here is because the wounded men roll right into our hands, in trains that have come down from close to the front line. We're the first port of call. We give the men something to eat and drink, clean them up, and maybe dress their wounds. Then on they go, to hospital in Rouen, or a convalescent camp in Havre. Or if they're lucky, they might be heading for a ship home.

There's another thing that can happen. They can die in the rest station, and they're taken away to be buried.

It's an incredible place, full of people throughout the day and night. Full of noise and activity. All around, people are speaking English, which surprised me at first, but there are very few Frenchmen here. This place seems to belong to the British Army now, and the few remaining Frenchmen are either very old, or young boys. The rest are away. Fighting. Those that are here work as orderlies and porters, like the old man who runs the platform. He's in charge of his own little army, composed mostly of boys, and they work continuously, and efficiently. The station is now a station and hospital combined, and runs very smoothly from what I have seen. There's even a tiny track on the platform itself along which runs a small wooden truck, to move supplies and medicine from one end of the platform to the other. All day long the Frenchman shouts at his boys who scurry about on the truck, taking rides and fooling about when they think no one's looking.

I left Brighton last Monday. That was the twenty-sixth, but first I had to prepare my escape.

*E*scape it was. I knew there was no way to tell my parents what I was going to do. All I could do was post a letter before I left Brighton. It will scandalise them, and their acquaintances, when they discover their daughter has vanished, but I cannot help that. This is a difficult world now.

On the Sunday before I left I had to undertake the first part of my plan. A small mission without which none of what I have achieved so far would have been possible.

It was Sunday, early evening. It was a warm evening, though not bright, but Mother didn't bat an eyelid when I said I was going out for a short walk.

'Take a coat,' she called from the kitchen. 'It looks like it might rain later.'

That was all she said, but how was she to know of the nervous beat of my blood?

'I've got one,' I said.

I walked out of the house and turned down to the seafront, but soon doubled back, by turning up Montpelier Road. There I was lost in the throng of people taking the evening air. I made my way to the hospital.

I carried my coat over my arm; hidden underneath it I had a canvas bag, neatly folded.

Though my heart was racing, I knew that my best chance of success would be to act as relaxed as possible, to project an air of confidence. So as I walked through the doors I simply nodded at the lady on the reception desk. I knew her by sight, and she knew who I was.

I half smiled.

'An errand for Father,' I said, by way of explanation, trying for all the world to sound bored and exasperated in equal measure.

It worked. I made my way up the central staircase, pretending to head for Father's office.

I did need something from his office, but I passed by its door. There was no light inside, as I knew there would not be. Father was out on the rounds with the other special constables, pestering people about obscuring their lights.

I made my way to the end of the corridor, then came down by the back staircase to the end of one of the wards, and there lay my goal. The laundry room.

The hospital was quiet that evening, which was my good fortune, but even so I checked up and down the corridor before I slipped inside.

For a moment I began to panic. The laundry room was full of sheets being washed, and blankets, and pillowcases. I could see uniforms too, but they were the wrong sort. There were plenty of regular nurses' uniforms, but I needed a VAD one. In fact, I needed both an indoor uniform, and the heavy, brown outdoor uniform too.

Frantically I began to hunt through the piles of clean uniforms, but couldn't find what I needed. In desperation I looked around and saw the basket for uniforms waiting to be washed. I rummaged through it and at last pulled out a couple of long, grey VAD uniforms. Then I found various aprons, each emblazoned with a red cross.

A thought occurred to me. I held up one of the dresses, but I couldn't be sure.

I looked at the door; there was no lock on the inside. Instead, I wheeled a huge laundry basket over to the door and jammed it up against the handle.

Quickly I stripped and tried the first dress on, and was glad I had; it had been made for someone larger than me and I looked silly. I would be spotted in a moment. Fumbling, I pulled it off and stuck my arms into the second dress. It was fine. I pulled it off again, and put my own back on. I stuffed the uniform into the canvas bag, along with the cleanest apron I could find, and a couple of caps.

I couldn't see an outdoor uniform anyway, and decided I would have to just wear my coat and risk it.

I pulled the laundry basket back into place, put my ear to the frosted window, and slipped out again.

Still I saw no one as I walked back to Father's office.

I tried the door, and to my relief it wasn't locked. This was a hospital, not a prison, after all.

I hurried inside.

I stood there undecided, and then started to hunt.

I knew my Father was responsible for passing and processing the volunteer nurses selected to go to France. On my last visit to his office, when we'd tried and failed to have tea, I'd seen a big box file on his desk that contained, I hoped, my ticket to France.

It was still there, labelled: Joint War Committee, Service Abroad.

Inside were several bundles of papers, each one concerning a nurse. I began to leaf through them. The first few only had the preliminary applications in them – that the nurse had put her name on the register to serve abroad. That she'd been notified of selection, that she'd applied for her passport, and so on. These were of no use to me. I rifled through to the end of the box. They were all the same, I tried to stay calm as I searched the desk, and then, in Father's out-tray, I saw another bundle, just like the ones I had been looking at. He must have been working on it on Friday night; it was a completed set of papers.

I grabbed it and checked it through.

The nurse selected was called Miriam Hibbert. I didn't know her, and I didn't want to, in a way. I was about to severely impede her means of going abroad.

Everything I needed was there. Her completed contract of service. The brassard armband with its red cross. An identity disc. An identity certificate. A 'red permit', that allows travel abroad.

And then the passport.

My heart sank. I hadn't seen a passport before then. Until the war started we didn't need them. I didn't know they had photographs. I looked at the small black and white image of Miriam Hibbert. She looked nothing like me. There was no getting around it. How could I pass myself off as her, with that tiny picture to prove it was all a lie?

Not wanting to give up, I looked at the identity certificate.

The Anglo-French Hospitals Identity Certificate was a small paper document. And it had no photograph.

On it I read that it could stand in place of a passport where none was present. I didn't know quite what that would mean in practice, but my heart soared. The certificate had the most basic information on it. Name, address, age, height. Again, my

140

luck held. Miriam was just an inch or two shorter than me, at five feet six, and she was twenty-three. I could pass for twenty-three. Then there was a brief, rather blunt description of her.

Tall, round face, brown eyes. Medium build. Straight, dark brown hair, to just above shoulder length.

It fitted me apart from the round face and medium build. Well, I could tell them I'd lost weight. And the hair – but I could cut that easily enough.

It was time to go, but just as I was sliding the papers on top of the uniform in my canvas bag, I saw a book I recognised on Father's desk.

On impulse I picked it up and slid it into the bag along with everything else.

The blood was still chasing round my veins twice as fast as it should, even when I was halfway home. All the way I expected to hear running footsteps coming after me, or cries of 'Stop! Thief!', but none came, and eventually I began to realise that I had done what I set out to do. I had my passport for France tucked up in a canvas bag under my arm.

As I reached the Seven Dials I stopped in a doorway and took out the book.

Miss Garrett's copy of *Greek Myths*.

There was no doubt. There, on the flyleaf, was her juvenile signature.

The book had made its way back into my possession. Mother had pushed it into Miss Garrett's hands as she'd left on that awful night over six months ago. Had she sent it to Father? She must have done, but why?

There was a piece of paper folded inside the book, and I wondered if it was a letter from Miss Garrett, explaining her reasons for sending it, but it was not. It was some official letter of Father's, that he was using as a bookmark. And if he were using it as a bookmark, that meant he was reading the book. I put the letter back between the pages where it had been.

For the first time since I decided to leave, I began to doubt myself.

I have the book with me now, as I sit in the canteen on this Saturday morning. It was a hazy start but it's clearing up now. In front of me is a bowl of porridge and tea in an enamel mug. All around are the smells of war and the smells of medicine. I have kept the book in the large pocket of my uniform since it came back to me. At first I saw it as an omen about home, telling me to stay. Then, more worryingly, I saw it as a link from me to Cassandra herself, and I was scared by that. But in the end I decided that it could only mean good luck, that maybe Father was trying to understand me at last. So I brought it with me to France.

With a shock I suddenly realise that today is Tom's birthday. I look up and around me. No one is looking at me, no one knows who I am. No one here knows Tom. I have no idea where he is. For a moment I feel very lonely, but it passes.

I raise my tea to my lips and whisper.

'Happy birthday, Thomas.'

Sitting here, feeling the weight of the book in my pocket, I allow myself to dwell on my last few hours at home.

When I got home with the uniform I went straight to my

room. Father was still out and Mother was sewing in the drawing room.

Coming downstairs again, I forced a yawn, and muttered something about an early night.

Mother looked up at me.

'Fine, dear,' she said, smiling weakly. 'You need plenty of rest.'

I didn't agree, but that's what I had been hoping she'd say.

'I'll take a drink up with me,' I said, and turned to go.

Mother didn't answer, but dropped her head back to her sewing, straining her eyes by the light from the standard lamp behind her.

I was struck by the sight of her. She looked like a painting, a woman at her sewing in the half-light, her husband out in the evening somewhere, one son dead, the other away at the war. For the first time in my life I realised my mother was an old woman, and I felt like crying.

I stood gazing at her for a long time, but she was so lost in her thoughts that she didn't even notice. The feeling of sadness inside me welled up so powerfully that I thought I would crumble. I looked at her one last time, and closed my eyes, trying to fight the feeling that I would never see her again.

I closed the door.

I slept, and I slept surprisingly well, until, at four in the morning, my alarm clock went off right beneath the pillow under my head.

It was time to leave.

*I*t may be summer, but it is still dark at four in the morning, and since Daylight Saving Time started back in May, it's darker for an hour longer in the mornings.

The darkness would help me later, but in my bedroom I fumbled for the things I'd prepared the night before. I had my case that I used for holidays, small, but strong. Everything I needed fitted into it, including the uniform, wash things and Miss Garrett's book. I took all the money I had, as well as everything from Cook's housekeeping jar in the kitchen. I felt bad about that, but I knew Father would replace it.

It was a fresh morning. I knew there was a train for Folkestone at five, so I had plenty of time, though there was something I had to do first. I hurried down to the station, praying that I would see no one I knew, but I needn't have worried. It was still dark, and besides, no one of my acquaintance, or that of my family's, would be out at that time of the morning – a time only for thieves and tradesmen, or for people like me, with a long journey ahead.

At the station I headed straight for the public conveniences. There, I pulled off my clothes, and changed into the VAD uniform. I put the clothes I had been wearing and Miriam

Hibbert's passport into the bag, and shoved it up on top of the cistern, where it was out of sight.

I pulled out a little mirror and the scissors I had brought, and considered my hair. It was straight, and easy enough to cut, though when I'd finished I saw what a mess the back was.

I tied my hair in a bun and hid the whole thing under my nurse's cap. I took my case in my hand, and left.

I waited at the far end of the platform for the train, and by five past five, Brighton was left far behind me. My journey had begun.

I thought of my parents, still asleep in their bed, unaware that with every passing minute I was a mile further from them.

I thought I had planned my journey in detail, but on the train that morning I began to think of all sorts of new things.

I knew that the hospital ships sailed from Folkestone to Boulogne, but had I fully understood what I was walking into, I might not have been so brave.

Then there was the question of passports. I hoped the identity certificate would be good enough.

As the train rattled into Kent I remember thinking I might have to give the whole thing up, or I would be stopped and sent home, in disgrace. Maybe they'd even think I was a spy trying to get back to Germany. The papers had been full of stories of people being arrested as spies, although most of them were probably totally innocent.

I got off the train at Folkestone with little clue where to go or what to do, but then I saw another girl in a VAD uniform smiling at me. She came over. I began to panic. I should give the whole thing up, and go home to face the shame and anger of my parents.

'Are you lost, too?' she said.

I nodded.

'I was, but I've got it all sorted now. I'm off to Boulogne. Are you?'

147

Without thinking I told her I was and then, of course, she wanted to talk to me.

'What's your name?'

I hesitated for a moment.

'Miriam,' I said. 'Miriam Hibbert.'

'Where are you from?' she asked, after she had introduced herself. Her name was Amelia, but she told me to call her Millie.

'Brighton,' I said. I didn't want to be rude, but I couldn't afford to give too much away.

We made our way down to the docks, and soon we were in a queue of people, mostly soldiers returning to the front, all waiting at the gate in the docks. It was about mid-morning by then, and the boat was due to sail at noon. It was a hot, bright day, and the queue was long. Millie smiled as the seagulls cawed and screeched above our heads. The boats in the harbour sounded their horns from time to time, and we could smell the salt in the air.

In spite of everything, in spite of my fear, it was thrilling.

Millie chatted as we shuffled slowly forward.

'How old are you?' she asked. 'I'm twenty-three.'

'I'm twenty-three, too,' I lied, but she just laughed and I smiled. After that she chatted away merrily, and asked fewer questions. I learnt a lot about her, without having to tell her much about myself, except that I was a VAD nurse from Brighton and had volunteered to go to France.

She'd been working in London and decided she wanted a bit of adventure, as she put it, so had put herself forward for service overseas.

I realised from what she said about her home that she was from a very wealthy family, but found life rather boring. This was her way of 'having an adventure' in a manner that her parents could not object to.

I watched Millie closely as we chatted. She was quite pretty, I thought, though some of her prettiness was down to having money to spend. I felt mean for thinking that, and tried to listen more attentively. She had a small, round mouth with lips that flew as she nattered about this and that, and deep brown eyes, like mine. I decided I liked her, and I thought I could trust her. Not with the whole truth, but with some of it at least.

'Millie,' I said, when she stopped for a moment.

'Yes,' she said, 'What is it?'

'I have a problem, but I wonder if I can ask you to help me?'

'What is it?'

'It was so early when I left this morning, I forgot things. I forgot my passport.'

'Oh!' she said. 'Oh, no. And what about your letter?'

'Letter?' I asked.

'From your hospital? You need a letter of authorisation for transfer from the commandant of your detachment at home. Don't tell me you don't . . . ?'

'Oh yes,' I said, quickly, 'Yes, I've got that. And my identity certificate.'

She looked at me, exasperated, but then smiled.

'Don't worry!' she declared. 'I'll get you through. As for your passport, well, either they need nurses out there or they don't!'

And she was right.

We got to the front of the queue to find a woman in civilian clothes but wearing a red cross on an armband. There was a sailor there too.

Millie had such an air about her as she explained my

predicament, and flourished my identity certificate, that in no time at all we were making our way up the gangplank on to the deck. It seems that passport controls are much more about stopping people from coming into the country than letting them leave.

The ship was a vast thing, almost a liner, which had been converted into a Red Cross hospital ship. It was painted white with a large red cross on each side, and we learnt that it spent its time crossing the channel, bringing the wounded home, and returning with supplies of all kinds, as well as new nurses, like us.

We set sail.

45

The crossing seemed to take a lifetime. Millie assumed that we were going to stick together, and I have to admit I was glad of her companionship.

Besides, without her I would probably have been on my weary way home.

It was a smooth crossing, but even so, I felt a little queasy.

'You'll feel better if we get some air,' Millie said, and since it was a warm day, I agreed.

We found a sheltered spot on one of the fore decks, and settled down, using our cases as seats.

'I wonder if I can get us a drink,' she said, and before I could answer, she was up and away. She is so bright and full of life.

'Watch my things, Miriam, please?'

I smiled as she went. She made everything seem easy, and I wondered if maybe it was. Maybe life was easier than I made it.

She was gone a long time, and I took the copy of *Greek Myths* from my case and began to read.

Out of curiosity, I opened it at the place Father had been reading, and felt a stab of regret shoot through me again.

Cassandra. He had reached a page that talked about Cassandra.

I read for a while, but the motion of the ship, the warmth, fresh air, and my tiredness all caught up with me. I must have fallen asleep.

At least, that is what I imagine, for only that can explain what happened next.

I was no longer Alexandra, in 1916, but another girl, long, long ago. I was on a ship still, making a fateful journey, but it was a warmer sea that my boat was crossing, and the boat was moving under sail and oar, not coal and steam. A ship that left the waters of the Hellespont, with the battered walls of Troy far behind, to head out across the Aegean.

As the ship reeled across the heaven-blue sea, I suffered as that other girl suffered. Abducted from my home by the violence of a foreign king, I prophesied not only his death, but my own as well, and despite the heat I shivered at the pain of a storm of things foreshadowed and foreseen.

The worst of it, as ever, was that no one would believe me.

My every utterance was taken to be worthless, the rantings of a mad woman. Yet I *knew* the truth for what it was, and it was coming to meet me faster than I thought possible.

The seagulls wheeling above my head should have told me we were approaching the French coast, but as I gazed at them, they were transformed into ravens. They flapped blackly around the boat, calling to me, mocking me.

You should know the future only when it has come; to know it before is grief too soon given. All will come clear in the sunlight of the dawn.

The boat drove on through the breaking waves.

By late afternoon the French coast was in sight. The sunshine of Folkestone had vanished, and a heavy rain beat down on us from a black sky. Our ship had to wait while a troop ship manoeuvred in the harbour, and so it took slow turns up and down the coast for an hour or more.

When Millie had finally returned with a bottle of lemonade, she took one look at me and decided I was unwell. I think I was no more than tired, but she feared something worse, and dragged me into the ship's galley where once again she had no trouble in making everyone do as she bid.

Before long I was sitting with my feet up in an officer's berth, a glass of ice water in my hand. This was not the quiet, unobtrusive arrival I had planned, but I couldn't stop Millie, and in any case, I was in something of a mess.

By the time the boat docked I had recovered, and then there was no more waiting.

We stepped on to Boulogne quay, on to French soil. The whole journey had taken no more than twelve hours. As we made our way from the docks to the railway station, I wondered what was happening at home, in Brighton. My parents would have discovered that I had disappeared. It would be a day at least before my letter reached them. I had wanted to give myself that much of a head start, in case they came looking for me, and even when they did get it, I didn't think it would reassure them very much. I knew they would be sick with worry, and yet I felt detached, not just by the distance between us, but by my sense of purpose.

That evening Millie and I were put into our detachment. There are a dozen of us in all, with a superintendent and quartermaster above us, and a commandant above them. Our superintendent is called Sister McAndrew. She's tough, keen on discipline. When I told her I'd forgotten my outdoor uniform, she made me buy one from the stores.

She gave us each a booklet of rules, detailing how we have to behave in France. I tried my best to look interested, though I can't shift the feeling that none of this really applies to me. My disguise is a means to an end; I'm only here for one thing. Then I remembered that if I'm caught I won't be able to find Tom, and I started acting like a nurse again.

I saw Sister McAndrew looking at me hard, but I told myself it was only my imagination. I am Miriam Hibbert now.

Millie and I have been assigned to No. 13 Stationary Hospital, but we will spend a couple of weeks learning general duties in the rest station at the railway station.

It has been a baptism of fire.

43

*T*hey all have it.

All of them.

The trench-haunted look. An appalling weariness behind their eyes. Every single man that has passed through the rest station while I have been here, and there have been literally thousands of them, has exuded an awful aura of . . . of what?

Is it horror? Or fear? Pain or fatigue or shock?

It is all of these things. They don't talk about the trenches specifically; you pick up hints and notions and hear stories and rumours, but none of them talk about it directly. Yet there is enough to form a terrible picture of what they have witnessed, what has been done to them, what they have done to other people. That's what made me realise what it is about them.

They have lost faith.

They have lost their faith in what it is to be human. And so the smallest act on our part, not even of kindness, but of mere consideration, makes them so desperately grateful that it makes me want to cry.

I haven't seen much of Millie, despite the fact that we're in the same detachment. We have been so busy that we have had no more chance than to nod and smile as we have passed once or twice. When I do see her, though, I am still struck by her irrepressible nature.

As for me, I see death at every turn. I see these men like ghosts waiting to be born. Sometimes it is just a feeling I get as I am tending to one of them, a sad realisation that I am wasting my efforts in patching him up, because in another fortnight he'll be dead, anyway. Sometimes I get a vision, horribly real, impossible to ignore. Last time it happened I nearly gave my self away. As I washed a soldier I suddenly saw corpse worms crawling across his face. When I blinked and looked again they were gone. I realised that it had been a premonition of his death in a field somewhere in Flanders.

I began to shake, but managed to control myself, and no one suspected anything.

In one way, that is the worst part of it. I have had to control my reactions to my visions, for fear of exposing myself. I am assaulted by them almost every waking hour, and it makes me sick to admit it, but I have got used to it. Not completely, of course, but to a very large degree, I witness these walking ghosts and do not turn a hair.

If I do, I may lose the chance of saving Thomas.

Although we are VAD nurses in the rest station, and not regulars in one of the base hospitals, we have had more to do than mere domestic work.

Each ambulance train has been specially converted to hold over three hundred men on stretchers, as well as maybe another fifty or so sitting cases. At times, when trains have been rolling into the station every hour, we have been inundated.

As men arrive here by ambulance train, they may have been washed and had their wounds cleaned by the nurses on-board, if they weren't too busy. The doctors decide what will happen to them next; home, hospital here, or back to the front.

Of course, most of them hope that their wound is bad enough to get them sent home.

'Is it a Blighty one, Sister?'

You hear those words all day, on every side of you. Blighty is a word picked up from the Indian soldiers; it's derived from their word for British things. The men want a Blighty wound, to get themselves a Blighty-ticket, one of the little forms like luggage labels that we tie on to the wounded who are being sent home. On the brown-card ticket is a diagonal red cross as

157

well as all sorts of information. The man's name, of course. His army number, regiment, and the date and name of the hospital ship he'll be taking home. On the other side is the diagnosis, details of any treatment en route, his age, his religion, his length of service.

And the sister will be gentle with them, or maybe joke with them, anything than say bluntly that they're going back to the war.

'A Blighty one? No!' she'll say, laughing. 'Not that scratch!'

And when he complains, she'll maybe add something.

'Still, you never know, if you hang around here for three or four days, maybe the medical officer will have too many tickets to carry and we might persuade him to get rid of two on you!'

Two tickets, of course. For they are never issued except on the assumption that when the man is better he will be coming back to France to fight again. He may be injured, but that doesn't mean he's left the army.

Despite myself, and my intention to find Tom and leave France, I find myself being drawn in by the wounded men. It's not possible to remain impervious to the anguish all around. Already in my short week I have seen many cases of shell-shock. In these cases, the diagnosis on the tickets will say one of two things: shell-shock, or neurasthenia. I can't see the difference in the men themselves, and I believe it's really down to the view of the medical officer who writes the ticket. In brackets after the diagnosis, there are one of two letters: 'S' or 'W'. 'S' is for sick, as in from dysentery or pneumonia; 'W' is for wounded, when they've been hurt in action. For the shell-shock cases, sometimes they put 'S' and sometimes 'W', as if they can't decide if they're sick or wounded. It may seem a small difference, but it will mean a lot to the men when they get better. For wounded men receive an army pension, sick men do not. It makes me wonder at how easily the doctors seem to make these decisions.

I have not yet managed to get any news of Tom's battalion. The postcards he sent were as good as useless. They're not allowed to say anything about where they are, in case the letters fall into the hands of spies and give away secret army information. But Tom knew he was heading for Flanders before he left, and I don't have any reason to suppose otherwise. If his battalion is still there, then any wounded would almost certainly come to Boulogne, though there is a small chance they might be taken by canal to St Omer, and then Calais.

I have tried to check the regimental badge of every wounded man I can. Sometimes it's easy enough despite the mud, but sometimes . . . sometimes the uniforms are not just caked in mud, but ripped to ribbons, as well. From the wire. Then it's very hard to see anything, maybe hard even to tell which bit of clothing it is you're removing from your patient.

I've found no badges from the 20th Royal Fusiliers. In a way, that's good news, for though it means no news of Tom, it also means that maybe his battalion are in reserve, and not fighting at the moment.

I say I have had no news of Tom, and that is true. But I have seen him.

Last night I had the dream again, in which I see him being

shot. It was just as real as before, but briefer, and chilling in its detail.

The raven was there, cawing at me, mocking, as usual. I saw the gun that will kill Tom. It was so clear I could feel the cold metal of the gun barrel heat up as the bullet spun down it.

Tom was surrounded by huge, rough spikes sticking out of the ground, up into the air. I couldn't work out what they were, and everything went hazy.

It's Saturday morning, and I'm drinking my tea and trying to shake the vision of the dream from my head.

It's the first of July. Tom's nineteenth birthday. It's actually pretty quiet on the station today, and in the rest station, but all morning rumours have been running around that something big is happening.

Down the valley, in the Somme.

Those who claim to know say the big push has come, and that very soon the wounded will start arriving in numbers hitherto undreamed of.

So far, though, it's just distant thunder.

*T*he last few days have flashed past, like the blurred view from a speeding train.

How quiet it seemed on Saturday morning. It wasn't long before that peace was shattered and we knew it had merely been the calm before the storm.

The big push had finally come.

Although many of the wounded are taken to the base hospitals at Rouen, directly down the line from the Somme valley, just as many of them come up to us via Abbeville or St Pol.

Millie and I were on the same shifts, and that day alone we must have processed a thousand men through our rest station. Next day was twice as bad, and there has been no respite.

It has been a continual onslaught, and it amazes me that we have coped, but we have. All day and night we take men in on their stretchers, direct from the train, clean them up, move them on. We load the trains with supplies for their next journey: clothes, cases of sterilised milk, butter, eggs, biscuits, meat extracts, cigarettes. Over and over and over again, until we are not even conscious of our actions any more. There are men everywhere. Bodies asleep in every conceivable corner of the station. And we keep working until every last one has been seen, and the station is quieter again. Then the next train arrives.

I have barely had a chance to think of Tom. Of course at first I worried continually, and all the while expected to see him being carried into our suite. I have heard of stories like that. One of our nurses saw her own brother being brought in. He had died on the train. It might seem extraordinary, but with the thousands of men coming through here, sooner or later things like that are bound to happen. She was inconsolable, but next day she was back, working again. Her world had changed, but it changed nothing. She still has a job to do.

After a while, I stopped thinking about Tom, though from force of habit I kept checking regimental badges, and I have seen none from the 20th.

Then, yesterday, Tuesday . . .

It was a horrible day, rain lashing down in angry bursts. The sky was brutally dark and it was hard to believe it was July. We could hear thunderstorms inland. At least, we thought they were storms, but sometimes we have heard the sound of the guns from the front. The big guns.

I handed a heavy bucket to Millie, and paused briefly to straighten my aching back, when the sister we were with crossed herself.

She was looking through the window of our surgery on to the platform. A shadow passed by. A dispatch rider stuck his head into the room, as if looking for someone. When she saw him, Sister looked away hurriedly, and bent her head to clean the rough wooden table we used to operate on.

He was gone almost as soon as he'd arrived, and Sister crossed herself again, shuddering.

163

'What is it?' I asked, 'What's wrong? Do you know that man?'

'No,' she said. 'And I don't want to. Everyone knows who he is.'

'I don't,' I said. 'What's wrong?'

She looked at me briefly, then started working again.

'Hoodoo Jack. That's what they call him. He's a bad wind and you should stay away from him.'

'Buy why? What's he done?'

'It's not what he's done, it's what he says. Used to be a soldier. Then he started to know when his mates were going to get it. He was right once too often. Went crazy. He's a jinx. That's why they call him Hoodoo.'

She crossed herself a third time, and would say no more.

39

I knew immediately that I had to talk to Hoodoo Jack, but two days passed before I got the chance. In that time there has been nothing but work. I am so tired. I looked in a mirror last night and hardly recognised myself. My face is sunken, my eyes are dull, my hair is lank, my skin grimy. My hands are sore from all the washing. Washing men, washing clothes, washing myself.

I saw my first gas cases yesterday. The first since . . . that man . . . in the hospital. Simpson. I tried not to think about him, but it all came back to me. What a different world the Dyke Road Hospital seems to me now. Even its makeshift nature was luxury compared with the primitive rooms we work in here. The floors are scrubbed, but they're still bare. The walls are whitewashed, and we put flowers in jugs, and keep it all as tidy as we can, but there's no forgetting that the rest station is just four primitive rooms in a French railway station.

There were three gas cases. Two privates and a corporal from a Scottish regiment. Their skin was blistered and burnt by the gas, and one of the privates couldn't see. None of them could talk, but they didn't need to.

I saw it all from them.

165

The dark fumblings in the early dawn.

'Gas!' someone called down the line.

I could see their wretched attempts to pull their gas masks on, and though they managed it in the end, they were too slow. The gas was borne in on a westerly wind, clinging to the ground, seeping into every crevice, unseen. The corporal got it worst, because he stopped to help his two young soldiers.

As he did so, he could hear his sergeant shouting at him.

'Always put your own mask on first. You won't be able to help anyone if you're dead!'

He heard his sergeant's words, though his sergeant had been dead two weeks by then. But he couldn't help it. He had to help the privates, they reminded him so much of his own boys at home. Thank God, at home.

I didn't see any more. I couldn't move. I was useless for five minutes, till Millie hissed at me. I'd never seen her angry before.

Afterwards she told me. Sister McAndrew was staring at me from the door. I forced myself back to work. I cut the men's clothing, and prepared them for departure to No. 13 Stationary.

And they were gone. Another three among the thousands I have seen. But I hope to God that poor corporal sees again.

The others don't seem to complain, so I dare not. I know I'm not really a nurse, but no one else knows my secret, not even Millie. I've always wanted to be a nurse, but I know now I was naïve. I had no idea what it would be like. I can't do this.

I can't tell anyone, but I long to. To grab someone and scream at them, that I'm not a nurse, that I don't know what

I'm doing, that I'm not strong enough to cope with all the horror around me. That I want to go home.

But I cannot. I think of Tom, and I cannot.

38

Later on, after the gas cases, I went out with Millie. The canteen was full of noise and people, and though our legs were crying out for us to sit down and rest, we took a mug of tea out on to the platform.

'Let's walk,' Millie said.

The station is massive, busy and noisy around the centre of the platforms and the buildings, so we headed for the far end. It's from that direction the trains roll in from the front, and yet, for the time being, everything was quiet.

Something made me think of Edgar. I was angry with him; he'd said I was useless and weak. Then I felt guilty because I remembered that he's gone.

I thought of Tom. It's almost overwhelming sometimes, and I don't know which is harder to cope with. The fact that Edgar's dead, or that Tom's still alive, but could be killed any day.

Millie and I had nearly reached the end of the platform. The rails ran off in front of us, away through Boulogne, away into the countryside, through towns and villages, through cuttings and clearings, until somewhere, the track must come to an end, maybe just a mile or two behind the front lines. I could smell cordite, though I have never seen a gun fired in my life; I could hear the shouts of battle.

Suddenly I realised Millie was gazing at me.

'How old are you really?' she said.

'I told you.'

She looked at me, dropped her head on one side.

'How old are you?' she said, gently.

'Eighteen.'

'And you're not a nurse are you? Not really.'

For a second I tried to act offended, surprised, but there was no point. She knew.

'No,' I said. 'Not really.'

'Who are you, Miriam?' she asked. 'What are you doing here?'

'My name's Alexandra,' I said, slowly. 'I've come . . .'

'No!' she said, suddenly. 'I don't want to know.'

I must have looked hurt, because she softened, then.

'I mean, it's probably better if I don't. I can guess, anyway. You've come here to look for your sweetheart, you want to get married before he . . . before . . . well, something like that.'

'Yes,' I said. 'Something like that.'

Neither of us spoke then. A minute passed.

I looked at Millie and smiled.

'How did you know?'

'Just a feeling. You're too young, though I don't think anyone's too worried about that. And your nursing. Have you had any training at all?'

I shook my head.

'I was a VAD for a while. I've spent some time in hospitals. My father . . .'

She held up her hand again.

'Don't tell me,' she said, but she was smiling. 'In that case,

169

you're doing really well, but to a trained eye it's obvious once you stop to look.'

There was no point denying it, but her words cut me. I thought I'd been doing well, but if it was that obvious I was an impostor, my chance of saving Tom could be snatched away at any time.

'I'll help you, if I can,' Millie said.

She put her hand on my shoulder, and without thinking I turned into her arms. I cried, quietly. Then I pulled away.

'I'm ruining your uniform,' I said, and we laughed, though it was a short, bitter laugh. Her uniform was already a mess from the day's work, the grey flannel stained with red blood, bright and fresh.

'Millie,' I said, 'You won't say anything . . . ?'

'No,' she said, 'I won't, *Miriam*. I believe you're here for a good reason, and anyway, you're helping the wounded. Don't be too hard on yourself, you're doing a good job. But I've noticed, and it's only a matter of time before someone else does. I have to tell you, I think McAndrew's got her eye on you. Be careful.'

I nodded, and tried to smile, but I couldn't. I physically couldn't.

'We'd better get back to work,' she said.

We turned to walk back to the hustle and bustle of the rest station.

A train was rolling in.

*S*even ravens fly about my head.

Whirling, whirling, their gun-black feathers beat the air, making a drumming in my ears that doesn't stop, but is transformed into the sound of cannon fire.

Their beating becomes more frantic, until, as I gaze upwards, a single black feather falls down to me, spinning like a sycamore seed on its way to earth.

The feather falls straight towards my face, and I try to lift my hand to catch it, but my arms will not move from my sides. The feather strikes me and brushes gently across my eyes.

Everything goes black.

I am sitting down. I can move my hands now and I feel a desk in front of me, like a school desk, but I am drowned in blackness.

From somewhere in the darkness, someone is suddenly shouting at me. It's hard to recognise the voice, because the words are Greek. I think it must be Miss Garrett, but then I realise who it is.

It's me.

The other me wails the words, as if she is a demon, shrieking each line with barely a breath between.

She screams the last word at me.

The Iliad. I think. That was from *The Iliad*.

'Iliad,' I say.

Yes, I know that answer. Please don't ask me another.

But she is shouting and screaming at me again.

'*Who wrote it?*'

'Homer.'

Don't ask me another.

'*Why is it dark?*'

'Because of the war,' I splutter out, hurriedly.

I got that one, but please don't ask me another. Please, Because I don't know that I can get another question right.

And then?

And then . . .

She is screaming at me again.

'*Why is there war?*'

I have no answer.

'*What does it mean?*'

I have no answer.

'*And the raven?*'

'What?' I cry out, tears streaming down my face.

'*The raven! What does it mean?*'

'I don't know,' I sob.

I don't know, I don't know, I don't know.

There is a flash of light through the darkness, and a moment later a terrible bang, and I burst from my nightmare, sweating, crying, panting.

But alive.

*H*oodoo Jack.

I don't know what I was expecting, what I was hoping for, but it wasn't this.

I asked around, as innocently as I could, though to be honest no one suspected my interest in Jack was anything other than food for gossip.

He had turned down a commission as an officer, but had become a corporal. Something happened to him and he ended up as a dispatch rider. Dispatch riders get away with a certain degree of freedom, even though they have messages to ferry around. Maybe that suits him better, being on his own much of the time. I understand that.

Every evening, I've lingered after my shift, hoping he would come by again. This evening, as I was leaving, barely able to keep my eyes open, I saw him walking down the platform, straight towards me.

I stopped in my tracks, and stared at him until he was close enough to touch. Then I realised I was being rude and looked away, embarrassed. He must have seen me, but he took no notice and walked past.

I turned.

'Jack?' I called, quietly. 'Excuse me.'

He didn't even turn his head, but walked on into the rest station.

I felt a fool, and then I felt angry, and then I decided not to let the chance go.

I waited for him to come back, and I didn't have to wait long.

I went straight up to him.

'You're Jack, aren't you,' I said, firmly.

He still ignored me and kept walking. I ran after him.

'Hoodoo Jack,' I said.

He whirled round and for a moment I thought he was going to hit me. He didn't have to, his eyes did enough damage.

I don't know what I'd been expecting. He isn't middle-aged yet, but he isn't as young as lots of the men I've seen here. There's something about him that doesn't fit. Something that says leave me alone. And whoever's in charge of him hasn't pulled him up on his stubbly chin, or filthy boots. His face is round, his eyebrows thick, and his skin is dirty.

'I'm sorry,' I said. 'I just . . .'

'Don't call me that,' he snapped.

'I'm sorry,' I said, again.

He didn't reply, but brushed past me.

I followed.

'I'm sorry,' I said, yet again, 'I just want to talk to you.'

'Very funny,' he said, not slackening his pace.

I scampered along beside him. We'd reached the end of the station. I guessed he was heading for the gate where I could see a motorcycle leaning against the railings.

'Wait,' I said, 'I want to talk to you. Really.'

'That's what they all say,' he spat out. 'Then, when I've told them a few stories, they have a good laugh.'

'No, I . . .'

'You're all the same. Stupid ignorant little bitch of a nurse.'

'No!' I shouted.

He stopped, and for the first time, looked at me.

'I'm not a little . . . bitch,' I said. 'I need to talk to you.'

He was a few strides from his motorbike.

'Wait! Please!' I was getting desperate.

He reached the motorcycle and swung his leg over it.

'I see things!' I shouted, not caring if anyone else heard.

He hesitated, briefly, looking at me for a second time.

'Please believe me,' I cried. 'I see things. I need to . . .'

But my voice was drowned by the roar from his engine as he spun it to life. He twisted his wrist and whirled away from me, dragging the back wheel around in the dust, and then speeding from the station.

'Please,' I said, though by then he was long gone.

35

It's Thursday evening. It's been raining all day, and I am exhausted. The business with Hoodoo Jack was the final straw. I know he'll be back soon – he's an RAMC rider and is around Boulogne all the time, going from hospital to hospital. I'll try to speak to him again. He can only tell me to go away.

Millie's sneaked off into town with a couple of other nurses, though if they're caught they'll be sent home.

I don't want to take the risk. Millie didn't protest when I said I didn't want to come. She could see I'm dead beat.

'Get some sleep,' she said. 'You need it.'

Then she gave me a kiss on the forehead, as though I was her little sister, and left.

I'm lying on my bunk in our billets in Wimereux, but I don't want to sleep. Sleep only brings dreams.

I think about the day.

The men. The pathetic men.

There is nothing noble in a suppurating, festering wound, and I wish Father were here to see that.

Then there are the cases of hand and foot wounds. They say lots of these cases are probably self-inflicted. Sometimes soldiers shoot themselves in the foot during a raid, hoping it will give them a nice, safe ride back home. Some of the nurses treat any men with these injuries contemptuously. But no one knows how they came by their wound; whether they're lying or not.

In the stationary hospitals they say men put dirty coins into their wounds to stop them from healing, so they won't have to go back to the fight. I don't know if that's true.

Today I treated a man who had two fingers missing from his left hand. I don't know what happened to him; I saw nothing. But if things were so bad he was prepared to shoot a couple of fingers off to get out of it all, then I can only feel pity for him, and shame. The shame of it all.

As the men arrive from the front we have to sort the wounded and to try to keep them from dying before they get their treatment. We are so over-stretched here, that there are not enough doctors to go around. Things were so bad at one point that Millie and I were sorting the dying from the nearly dead. Those who had a chance from those who had none. Life was leaking away from many of them, I could feel that, but we had no way of knowing which man needed treatment immediately, which could wait. We had to decide for ourselves, there was no one to tell us.

Sometimes I got a vision from the man I was treating, and that made me wonder if there was any point in helping them at all. What is the point in saving someone now, for them to be killed in a month's time? But then I realised. If I decide to pass by a man because I know he's going to die soon anyway, what does that say about what I am trying to do for Tom?

We are playing God, but we are weaker gods. Imperfect, unknowing gods. Gods that get things wrong.

But at the time we thought nothing of the sort. We did our

best, I suppose, judging from their coldness who was too far gone, who might have a chance.

Day after day we cut off bandages to reveal stinking wounds that have rearranged the whole idea of a man's body. A picture comes to me as I lie here in bed.

I see myself gazing mesmerised at the chaos, the men on stretchers on the floor, the heaps of discarded boots and mud-caked clothing, the cheap blankets, the smashed bodies and filthy blood-stained bandages. An unbearable stench rises from the appalling horror that waits underneath the cotton wool, and at one point the only equipment that I had for dealing with it was a pair of forceps standing in a glass jar half-full of meths.

I'm just a girl in a nurse's uniform, but that doesn't mean I know how to save these men, and them – they are men in uniforms, but that doesn't mean they know how to die.

34

*T*ime is running out.

That's true for me, it's true for so many out here. I hope it will not be for Tom, but I don't feel like praying. Although I would not say it aloud, I don't think God is listening anymore.

My time is running out. My money is running out.

The V in VAD stands for voluntary, with good reason. We don't get paid. That's why VAD nurses are from wealthy backgrounds, or have private means of some sort.

I looked at how little money I have. Fortunately I don't need much here, but McAndrew made me buy an outdoor uniform. Of course we are fed, we have our uniforms and a roof over our heads, but that's it. If I leave here to find Tom, I'll have very little to live on.

Nor do I really have a plan for finding him. I've been here nearly two weeks, and haven't found a single soldier from his regiment. That was as far as my plan went.

And Sister McAndrew is on to me.

Thank heavens for Millie.

I don't know how she does it. She has boundless energy. I heard her come in late last night from the trip to town. She told me this morning that they'd found a café. There was music playing, and dancing. There were some Tommies there, who asked her to dance, but she refused. Instead she danced with the young French waitress, and they laughed and laughed until her father, who owns the café, told the girl to start waiting on the tables again.

Despite that, she was up for duty on time, whereas I could hardly drag my aching limbs from bed after another night of wretched dreaming. And she was ready for McAndrew.

We were seeing to another batch of men.

Sister McAndrew was with Millie, me, and a couple of other VADs.

She took one look at the men, and then barked at me.

'Nurse! Nurse Hibbert. Fetch the Harrison's.'

I didn't have a clue what she was talking about.

She rounded on me.

'Did you hear me, Nurse? The Harrison's pomade. Now.'

I dithered.

'You do know what it's for?' she asked, her voice slowing. I could sense her suspicion.

Millie cut in, saving me. She was playing innocent, I could see.

'It's for the lice,' she said, 'isn't it? Sister?'

McAndrew glared at her, then at me. Before she could open her mouth I decided to speak.

'I just don't know where we keep it,' I said.

'I do,' said Millie. 'I'll go.'

Millie, bless her, left for the store cupboard.

McAndrew gave me another hostile glare.

'Where did you do your training?' she asked.

'I . . . the Dyke Road in Brighton,' I said. I had to go along with what I knew about Miriam Hibbert. I had no choice.

'For how long?'

I saw my chance.

'I had the three months minimum,' I said.

'It shows,' McAndrew said, eager to take the easy jibe that I had offered her.

'I just wanted to come and help,' I said, trying to sound as pathetic as possible. It wasn't hard.

And then Millie was back with us, and started chatting to McAndrew about her days in London as if they were old acquaintances.

She saved me.

This time.

33

*A*fter my narrow escape with Sister McAndrew, I saw Hoodoo Jack passing the window of the dressing suite. I looked at Millie.

'Cover for me? Please?'

I begged her with my eyes not to question me.

'Don't be long!' she called, but I hardly heard her.

Jack slipped into a room further down the platform, and I followed him.

He was on his own, waiting to deliver a packet. He turned as I came in.

'You,' he said, without obvious meaning.

'You remember me?' I asked.

He grunted.

'I'm mad, not stupid.'

There was silence.

Then I broke it.

'I see things, too,' I said. 'I see when men are going to die.'

He looked at me with such disgust and hatred, that I felt I might wither on the spot.

The door flew open.

It was a captain; beyond him I saw other officers sitting around a desk.

The captain glanced at me, but didn't bother to ask why there was a nurse in his quarters. The place is a hospital of sorts, after all.

'That all?' he said to Hoodoo Jack.

'Sir,' he nodded, and handed over the packet.

The captain tried to take it from Jack, but he wouldn't let go. His fingers had frozen around it. I saw Jack staring at the captain, for a second, maybe two, no more.

'What are you doing, man?' snapped the captain, and Jack shook himself.

He muttered something under his breath, then, pulling himself together, saluted messily, turned and left the room.

Without knowing what I was doing, I grabbed the captain by the arm.

'What on . . . ?'

It was enough. I let my fingers slip from his tunic.

'Thank you,' I said, quietly, for I had seen all I needed.

I ran after Jack. I don't want to think of him as Hoodoo Jack, though. Not now.

I caught up with him.

'You saw that?' I said.

'Go away, girl.'

'You saw it. I saw it too.'

He hesitated before answering.

'You saw nothing.'

'You saw what I saw. The captain. Lying dead in a shell hole, with the back of his head gone.'

'No!' he shouted at me now, so loudly that I could see people around us staring.

I hadn't realised it but we were already back outside the

suite where I was supposed to be working. Millie stood in the doorway.

'Get in here,' she hissed at me. 'For pity's sake, before McAndrew comes back.'

Jack had gone.

I slunk in and got back to work.

Then, was it only an hour ago? He came to me.

I'd finished my shift, and was walking out of the station to catch a lift in a truck to our billets up on the hill at Wimereux.

I heard the low growl of a motorcycle behind me. I turned and saw, yes, Jack, coming up behind me at no more than walking speed.

He drew level, and I stopped walking.

'Do you know when?' he asked. 'When he's going to die.'

He was talking about the captain; the captain whose arm I'd touched. Whose death I'd seen.

'I . . . I don't know,' I said.

I was afraid that the slightest wrong move on my part would send him away, but he stayed.

'Tomorrow,' he said. 'By this time tomorrow, he'll be dead. Everything else will be just as you told me.'

It was enough to know that he believed me.

'Do you still want to talk?' he asked.

'Yes,' I said. 'Yes, I do.'

'Then get on, and we'll find somewhere quiet.'

He nodded at the metal luggage rack behind his seat on the motorbike.

'No . . .' I said. 'I can't. We're not allowed to . . . If anyone sees me, I'll be sent home.'

'Fair enough,' he said, and pulled his goggles down over his eyes.

'No!' I shouted. 'I'll come. But let's get away from here quickly.'

I got on, put my arms around his waist, and prayed to Heaven and Hell that no one would see me.

32

I don't think of him as Hoodoo now. Not now I know he's a person. A person just like me. Hoodoo is a name superstitious people gave him. A horrible label, that helps them to think he's a freak. Well, if he's a freak, so am I.

I don't know exactly where we went.

We rode out of Boulogne and into the rain. I had to pull my long skirts up to sit on the bike, and the seat was a tiny plate of metal. I rested my feet on the little pedals used to start the bike, but even so, I nearly lost my grip.

'Hold tight!' he shouted from in front, and I clung to him as tightly as I could.

We rode through some ugly villages, heading inland, until we came to one slightly larger, but no less down-at-heel.

'No one will know us here,' he said.

Not for the first time it crossed my mind that what I was doing might be very unwise. But I had no choice.

He stopped outside a seedy looking café. They call them estaminets. Inside it's sort of a bar, but they cook basic food, too. I had heard of them but never been in one. It looked awful. There was a beaten old piano in one corner, but no one was playing it.

The place was busy, but not full.

'Don't meet anyone's eye,' Jack said. 'And keep your coat done up. Nurses don't come to places like this.'

He pulled me along to a table by a wall in the quietest corner.

A young girl came over. I tried not to look at her, but I couldn't help it. She was very young, and very dirty, and when she spoke there were gaps in her teeth. She wiped her nose on the back of her hand and look at Jack.

'Monsieur?'

'Du vin,' he said. I didn't dare open my mouth to protest, and I knew my English accent would give me away, even if I spoke French.

The girl sloped off, and came back after an age with a jug of red wine and two glasses.

'Vous mangez quelque-chose?' she asked, but Jack waved her away, which was a pity, because I would very much have liked something to eat, even if it was the ropy stuff I could see on other people's plates. Especially if I was going to have to drink wine.

Jack poured us each a glass and I glanced at the other people in the room. Locals, I guessed, all old men, and a couple of boys; the sort with something wrong with them, or else they'd have been away fighting. There were soldiers at another table, but they took no notice of us. I didn't want to know what they might be thinking.

'How long?' Jack said.

'I never understand what you ask me,' I said, trying a smile. He didn't smile back.

'How long have you been seeing things?

I shrugged. I thought about Clare. But that was so long ago, and it had only happened once, then.

187

'Almost a year, maybe,' I said. 'How about you?'

'Pretty much from the start. Since I got here.'

He emptied his glass, and refilled it straight away.

I took a sip of mine, to show I could if I wanted. It was vile stuff, but that didn't stop Jack.

'It was nothing at first. Just a tingling. Like an itch from a mosquito bite. So faint you might be imagining it.'

'You were a captain, then?'

'Who told you that? No, I was never a captain. I turned down a commission, because I wanted to be one of the men. We're all out here to fight and I didn't see why I should have an easier time than the boys, just because of my background.

'I was a corporal then. But even corporals aren't supposed to indulge in that sort of thing. Superstitions. Of course, we lads in the trenches, we live by them. And die, too.

'We all have our little routines, for good luck. Which sock goes on first, maybe. Or something from a dead mate, a watch perhaps, that sort of thing. And it's bad luck to say something good without grabbing a bit of wood right away. The ones that are left alive think that just goes to show that their superstitions are working, and the ones that are dead can't argue back that theirs aren't.'

It was clear he wanted to talk now.

'So what happened, then?' I asked. 'When did it start to change?'

He finished another glass of wine, and I began to doubt that there was any chance of getting back to Boulogne safely.

'The itch became a scratch, one day.'

He tipped the jug up, drained it, then waved it in the air. The young girl brought a full one over.

She eyed us curiously, and I looked away. I drank some more, it seemed to help.

'All of a sudden,' he said, 'the itch was a scratch. It scratched me so hard that I jumped to my feet. And shouted.'

'What did you shout?'

' "Williams has got it." And the other lads in the trench looked at me as if I were a madman. Sit down, they said. Nerves getting, to you? they asked. Happens to us all, someone said. And then five minutes later, the news came down the line. "Lieutenant Williams is dead. Got his spine ripped out by a nose-cap." And that was that.

'I stood there, feeling sorry for the lieutenant. But it was no shock to me, you see, because I'd known it was going to happen. The lads stared at each other. I noticed that, straight away. They looked at each other, but none of them would look at me. And that was just the first time . . .'

'What happened?'

He didn't answer, but gazed at his wine, as if it were a looking-glass.

'I'm sorry,' I said, after a while, to fill the silence.

'It's all right,' he said. 'What about you? How does it happen for you?'

I told him how it had started slowly, like his itch. How it was coming clearer each time. I told him about the hospital, back at home in Brighton. I told him that people had seen things in my eyes, though I didn't know what.

I told him about Clare, and then I told him about Edgar.

'What's your name?' he asked.

'My real name's Alexandra,' I said. I could see no point in lying to him.

'Alexandra,' he said, carefully. He seemed to be thinking. 'And no one believes a word you say?'

I shook my head. I knew that if I tried to speak, I would start crying and maybe never stop.

'"*And soon you too will stand aside, to murmur in pity that my words were true.*"'

He was quoting at me, and I knew where from. Miss Garrett's book had not been wasted after all.

My heart was racing. He knew about Cassandra.

'And now?' he said.

Now, I thought. Yes, what now?

'Let me put it another way,' he said. 'What are you doing here?'

I hadn't told him about Tom.

'There's someone I have to find. I've seen his death.'

'Your boyfriend?' he said, without sympathy.

'My brother. My other brother.'

He laughed at me then, and I didn't like it.

'Do you believe it hasn't happened yet?

I nodded.

'I know it,' I said.

'And what are you going to do?' he asked. 'You, a girl, against the whole of the German army, and the British one, too? You're going to have to defeat them both to get him out of here!'

He cursed bitterly, and drank his wine.

I pushed mine away. I felt like throwing it in his face.

'I don't know what I'm going to do. I saw his death. I know it hasn't come yet. I'm going to try to find him. I'm going to tell him what I've seen, and I'm going to get him out of here. And no, I haven't the faintest idea how!'

190

I broke off.

People were staring at us. At me.

Jack looked at me, but more gently than before.

'I'm sorry,' he said.

'That's all right . . .'

'I'm sorry,' he said, 'but you don't understand. There's nothing you can do.'

'No,' I said, 'I'll find a way . . .'

'No,' he said. 'You don't understand. If you've seen his death, then that's it. It's going to happen. You've seen the future. You can't change it.'

His words cut me badly. I suppose I had known this deep down all along, but had tried to not let it surface. Now it was out in the open, and I couldn't ignore it.

'All those other times. You have seen deaths, and they have happened, because they were the future. What makes you think it will be any different with your brother? That's how it is. You should go home before you get yourself killed. Or worse. What are you going to do? Dress up as a man, as if this is some kind of fairy tale, and find him in the whole of the front line?'

I could feel tears falling from my face on to the table now.

'But that's . . .'

'Awful?' Jack said. 'Terrible? Terrifying? Appalling? Which is it to be? Because I've been through them all, and still can't decide which. The future is written, and there's nothing you can do about it. The future is written in blood. Your brother's death, yours, mine. All written and waiting to happen, and not a damn thing you can do about it!'

He flung his hand at the jug which smashed against the wall. The last of the wine flowed across the rough surface of the table, and I could not help but see it as blood that had been shed.

A large old man came across the room towards us. He looked angry. I guessed he was the owner. I could see the young girl peering at us from behind the bar. The soldiers, too; one of them stood up, sensing trouble.

But Jack averted it all.

He rose, took an extravagant bundle of francs from his pocket and put the notes on the table, avoiding the wine.

He held his hands up to the man, and shrugged, showing that we were leaving. Seeing the money, the man smiled back.

As we went Jack spoke to him.

'Je suis desolée,' he said.

And in my muddled state, I couldn't remember whether that meant 'I'm sorry' or 'I'm desolate', though I knew what Jack meant, in truth.

Jack seemed to sober up quickly. Maybe he was never anywhere near drunk, but he brought me back to Wimereux, where it was Millie's turn to be appalled at how late I was.

'Alexandra,' she whispered to me, through the darkness. 'I heard McAndrew talking about you. She was talking to our section superintendent. I didn't hear what they said, though. I just heard your name. Well, they said Miriam, but you know what I mean.'

I was too tired to care.

I'm lying in bed now, trying to remember everything Jack said. As he stopped the motorcycle, and helped me to the ground with a gentle hand, he spoke to me, softly.

'Alexandra,' he said. 'Try to understand that there's nothing you can do. The future has already happened. We're just waiting to live it.'

'Well, then,' I said. 'In that case, it's my future to try to save Tom, whether he dies or not.'

Jack smiled, thoughtfully.

'You're a wise girl. It took me years to get to that point. Very well, then it's my fate to tell you this. Your brother's brigade is in Flanders. Around the La Bassée canal. You can't miss it. There's a new crater near Givenchy called the Red Dragon that you could lose St Paul's Cathedral in. But you'd better hurry, no one stays in one place for too long around here.'

And he sped off in to the darkness, his engine roaring loud enough to wake the dead.

31

I dream.

I dream of Jack, his pale blue eyes, and I can see that once there was life in them, that once they showed joy. I see him as a young corporal, eager to please, prepared to work hard.

It's gone now, that blue fire in his eyes; they are eyes that have seen too much death and are dying from it themselves.

But not entirely.

I cling to the fact that even Jack, who has had all belief ground out of him, had enough spirit left to set me on my way to Tom.

I'm coming.

30

*F*ive days have passed since that evening with Jack, the longest five days of my life.

I thought I was coming to find Tom, but the war had other ideas. In a way it was the war that saved me, and the war that betrayed me.

The day after Jack told me where to find Tom I got even more definite news of his battalion. I had still not seen a soldier wearing the uniform of the 20th Royal Fusiliers, but I also knew that had there been any I might have missed them. There were still as many as thirty trains a day arriving, loaded with wounded.

We were stretched beyond exhaustion that Saturday, as we had been all the previous week. Most of the casualties were coming from the south, from the Somme, but there were one or two trains from the east, from Flanders, and that was where my attention was now fixed.

From the east there finally came the message I had been waiting for, but it was a grisly one.

A train rolled in from Bethune about nine o'clock that Saturday evening, and I set myself to help unload the wounded. There was such chaos and confusion along the platform that no one noticed that I should have finished my shift and left by then.

Finally I saw what I had been waiting for.

He had died on the train. A private of the 20th, a public school boy who didn't even look as old as Tom.

Shamelessly I cursed him for dying before I could question him, ask him where he'd come from, where the rest of the men were now. And if he knew Tom. But he must have done. I know that Tom's battalion is a small, close-knit one. It has a poor reputation, because it's very new, and it's formed only of boys from public school.

But the boy in front of me would be answering no questions.

Sisters and nurses were staggering wearily from the carriages, orderlies lifting the stretchers on to the platform. The men who could walk were shuffling down to the rest station.

I would have to be quick. The dead boy lay on a stretcher on the platform. It was obvious he was dead, but everyone was too busy worrying about those still living.

I put out my hand and touched his white face. I hate to say it but I have seen so much death now it leaves me cold. If I thought of every mother of every soldier waiting at home and praying, I'd break down. It's the same for all the nurses. We have become immune.

Nothing. He had gone, and whatever life is had gone with him. I felt nothing, saw nothing, heard no words.

Then I felt ashamed of myself, and came away, before anyone noticed that in spite of my precious immunity, I was crying over a dead boy who I'd never even met.

29

I went back to our billets, and slept.

Things were closing in on me last Sunday, though as I reported for duty that morning with Millie, I had no idea how fast.

It was another ominous, cloudy day.

Trains poured in constantly, and once more we waded through a sea of wounded men, and their bloody bandages, and muddied uniforms. Cutting, washing, daubing, wrapping.

Then we heard that there were shortages of nurses and doctors aboard the trains. It meant nothing to us at the time. There's a shortage of everyone and everything, everywhere.

Later that morning Millie heard that she was going to make a run on an ambulance train to Amiens and back. It meant she'd be away for hours, the best part of a day in fact, and then I was scared. I needed Millie, I needed her looking out for me, covering my back, keeping an eye on McAndrew.

It wasn't to be. Around lunchtime, she left on the train for Amiens. I didn't even see her go, or have time to say goodbye, because I was waist deep in mess in the rest station. At the time I just felt sorry not to have seen her go.

I had no premonition. I didn't know then what has happened since. I had no idea what was going to happen to me

197

later, and it made me aware of something I had not considered before.

In all the things I have seen, and witnessed; in all the foreshadowings, I have yet to see anything about myself.

The war saved me.

It was about ten o'clock on Sunday evening. I had been working for nearly fourteen hours without a break. I scarcely knew what I was doing.

Men came into the rest station, without ceasing. Man after man after man. Tall ones, short ones, thin ones, young ones. A few older ones, but not many. By then they were all the same to me. I hate that. When I got to France, I cared about every man, and I saw each as an individual with his own story.

Now, they're just men, and I treat them all the same. I have become blunted to them, I can no longer feel for them. But I sense their terror as a single, huge monster.

Occasionally, I see death in front of me on a living man's face, but even that no longer shocks me. I have seen it so much.

But every death reminds me of Edgar, and reminds me of Tom.

Suddenly I was plucked from the slow hell of the rest station dressing suite.

'Hibbert!'

I was so lost in my work, so exhausted, that I heard the name called maybe only the third time.

'Hibbert!'

Dimly I wondered who McAndrew was shouting at, then I saw the other nurses looking at me.

With a sickening fear I realized that it was me she was calling.

'Come with me,' she snapped.

McAndrew walked briskly down the corridor, until she reached the superintendent's office.

'In here.'

I went in, expecting to find someone waiting for me, but the room was empty.

McAndrew closed the door behind us.

'Who are you?' she said, her voice quiet now in the closed room.

I hesitated, tiredness fuddling my thinking.

'Miriam,' I said. 'Miriam Hibbert.'

'Don't lie to me,' she said, again quietly. She pulled a piece of paper from her pocket. A telegram.

'Just so you know there's no point lying,' she said, flourishing it in my face. 'I wired the Dyke Road on Friday. I've just received this reply. They say Miriam Hibbert is in England, some problem over her papers, it seems. So who are you?'

I was speechless.

All around me, and yet as if from a great distance, I could hear the noise of the rest station, of the railway station that it still was. I could hear shouts along the platform outside, the hiss of steam from the engines.

'So, you refuse to speak, do you?' McAndrew said. I couldn't

200

help noticing that she seemed to be enjoying this drama, 'Well, I have warned the Commandant of my suspicions. I'm going to fetch him now.'

She opened the door, taking the key from the lock. She paused, and looked at me.

'They shoot spies, you know,' she said, her voice full of threat.

Then she closed the door and locked it behind her.

A spy? Surely they couldn't think that I was a spy?

Of course, they could. I was silly and weak. I could almost hear Edgar telling me so. I had got into something way over my head.

Breathlessly, I waited.

I had no idea how long I waited, but as I said, the war saved me.

Outside on the platform, I heard a train getting ready to roll out of the station. Shouts came from the head of the line.

I heard footsteps running.

'Come on,' shouted a voice, teasingly. 'We'll go without you!'

McAndrew may have locked the door, but I suppose the police game was new to her. Either that, or it never crossed her mind that a young woman would do such a thing as climb out of window, even a young woman who's a spy.

But there was a window from the office on to the platform, and it was not locked.

I opened it a crack, and saw an RAMC doctor hurrying for the train.

'Bethune, then!' he shouted, leaping aboard. 'Here we come!'

Bethune.

From that moment on I didn't think.

Everything I did, I did with complete calm, and I swear not a further thought ran through my head.

Bethune. The train was heading for the casualty clearing station in Bethune, the nearest point to the La Bassée canal.

I opened the window fully, and looked up and down the platform. There were people everywhere; wounded soldiers, nurses, RAMC, orderlies. I ignored them all.

With a loud hiss and a heaving of pistons, the train started to move. As if it were the most natural thing in the world, I pulled a chair to the window, sat on the ledge, swung my legs over and dropped to the platform. I walked steadily but without panicking towards the train, and was in time to step calmly on to the last carriage as it passed me.

Avoiding any chance of being seen from the platform, I opened the carriage door, and went inside. I came face to face with a VAD sister, and although she was a sister, she looked only a few years older than me.

'Hello,' I said, smiling. 'They sent me along too.'

She nodded.

'I nearly missed my train,' I added, trying to make her laugh.

She smiled, but it was a thin, unfriendly smile.

'Very good,' she said. 'We need all the help we can get. Have you been on an ambulance before?'

I shook my head.

'Then I hope you learn fast.'

The train picked up speed, but was still travelling quite slowly, and I knew it probably wouldn't go much faster. Many of the trains are a mixture of carriages from different French railway companies, and I've heard that the tracks are patched up in places. It isn't safe to go very fast.

I settled down for the journey, with failing hope and little knowledge of what might happen to me, but I was sure of one thing.

There was no going back.

'What's your name?' the sister asked me.

'Alexandra,' I said, without thinking, but if the sister wondered why my face suddenly flushed, she didn't say anything.

'We use surnames here,' she said.

As she waited for me to reply it occurred to me that maybe it wasn't such a bad thing to have given my real name. If anyone was coming after me, they would be looking for a girl called Hibbert.

'Fox,' I said 'Sorry, Sister.'

She was a tall, well-built woman. From the white eight-pointed star on her apron, I saw she belonged to a St John's VAD unit, but I saw other nurses with the red cross on their uniforms, like me, and relaxed. But it made me realise there were so many tiny things which might give me away.

'There's not much to do on the way,' Sister said. 'It's the journey back that . . .'

She trailed off.

'Well, you'll see.'

'How long does it take?'

'Hours. It's barely fifty miles, but you see how slowly we're going. It's a long train, can't go that fast. Then sometimes we have to stop and wait for the line to be cleared. Or if there's an air raid.'

She called to the other nurse in the carriage.

'Nurse Goodall, this is Fox. Show her the ropes. She can help you with the brechots. Then you should both try to get some sleep.'

Nurse Goodall came over to me as Sister made her way through the connecting door to the next carriage.

'What's a . . . ?' I hadn't even heard what she'd said properly.

Goodall smiled.

'A brechot? See where the stretchers go? The brechot is the rack that holds them. We have to check they're all ready, with sets of clean sheets for when the men are brought in.'

I nodded.

'She's not so bad,' she said. 'Sister, I mean. She meant what she said about getting some sleep.'

After we had finished, we went along to the carriage at the end of the train set aside for nurses. There we lay down on the low bunks, and slept our way towards Belgium.

Towards the front, towards the war.

The lights in the carriage were low, the blinds were drawn, so that no light would show to enemy aircraft. This was a newer train, I could tell, because the lights were electric. The carriage even had radiators warmed by steam from the engine.

I lifted a blind, and peered out into the night. I could see nothing. No stars, no moon. I could only guess at the shape of the countryside through which we were moving.

The train rattled on, click-clacking over points from time to time, rocking us slowly into oblivion.

But I could not sleep, and I needed to talk.

Goodall was snoring gently opposite me.

I felt bad, but I couldn't stop myself.

'Wake up,' I said, shaking her shoulder gently. 'Wake up.'

After a while, she opened her eyes and lifted her head.

'What is it? Are we there?'

'No.'

'Then let me sleep, will you?'

'Please,' I said. 'I'm scared.'

She sat up.

'I know,' she said. 'So was I, first time.'

'How many times have you done this?'

'Once.'

'How close do we get, to the front line?'

'Depends,' Goodall said. 'Bethune Casualty Clearing Station. I think it's just a couple of miles out to the front at the moment. But listen, when we get there, you'll be so busy, you won't have time to be scared.'

I looked at my watch.

It had gone midnight.

'Go to sleep,' she said, 'We'll be there soon enough.'

She couldn't know about what was happening to me, about Tom. I wondered if we'd really be there soon enough.

I lay down on the bench seat again, taking my apron off to use as a pillow. It was softer than it had been – it had not seen starch for a long time by then, but still, it didn't make for comfortable rest. I had been working since early that morning, and I could stay awake no longer. My mind began to drift, but not at random. I felt it drift out ahead of us. I was on high, looking down at the steaming train, churning through the dark French air. Occasionally, the driver would stoke the boiler and I saw the orange flash of fire from the coal in the furnace.

If I looked I could see all the way back across the sea to England. Over the water, past the piers, to Brighton. Into my home. I could not see Mother and Father, I had no sense of them. I wondered what they were doing. I knew they would be worrying about me, but they would have no idea where I had gone.

Then, from somewhere ahead, I saw other, different flashes of light. After each one, came a thunderous rumble. I drifted on, far ahead of the train now, and began to feel the souls of those who had died and were dying.

It scared me, because I thought I was still awake. I pulled my mind back from what lay ahead and tried to form a plan. I had come straight from the rest station, with only the uniform I was wearing, with no money. When we got to the CCS at Bethune, I knew it would be pandemonium. There would be a chance for me to slip away if I wanted, but where to? With no money, and no idea how to find Tom.

And what about the men? I wasn't supposed to be on the train, but I was. If I was looking for Tom, it would mean turning my back on men I could help.

Somewhere along the line, I did sleep, and I dreamed. The sound of the train rumbling became the sound of wing beats. And there in my dreams, as I expected, the raven was waiting for me.

I was almost glad to see it, because I needed it to talk to me. I needed it to tell me what it meant, but it said nothing this time. It hopped around on the stump of a blasted tree, and flapped its wings. It cocked its head on one side and opened its beak, but no words came. It mocked me with its silence.

It told me nothing, and I woke, cursing it, still unable to understand why it keeps appearing to me.

And then I realised the train had stopped.

As I lifted the blind on the carriage window for a second time, my hand was trembling. It was early morning, and a weak, dawn light spread across the landscape.

I felt more alone that I have ever done in my life. We had trundled through the night, travelled east, inland, and reached the railhead at Bethune, being used as the casualty clearing station. It's a squalid little place, a drab provincial town suddenly made important because a war has happened to come by. I was watching the scene at the platform, when the door of our carriage opened, and Sister came back in.

'Right, you two. This is it. Look sharp.'

I forced myself to think. I had to decide what to do, and I had to decide quickly, but I was tired, and before I knew what was happening, the first of our men were being carried in on their stretchers.

The smell hit me first. They were fresh from the battlefield and reeked of death and disintegration. But as Nurse Goodall had said, there was no time to be scared. And there was no time to make choices. I had to help get the men stowed aboard. As soon as our carriage was full we began to cut their uniforms from the worst wounds where possible.

As I worked I began to talk to the men. After the initial

shock I gathered my wits. I had to take this opportunity, because if I went back, my time would have run out.

I asked each man I tended about Tom's regiment, but no one knew anything about it.

I felt desperate. Already the train was taking on new supplies of water and coal; as soon as we had everyone loaded, we would be setting off back to Boulogne. I would just have to slip off the train and take my chances.

Then, one of the last men aboard heard me talking to another soldier.

'I'm trying to find out where my husband is,' I was saying, thinking that might move someone enough to talk to me.

'You said he's in the 20th Royal Fusiliers?'

I turned and saw a man in the top of the brechot behind me. He was in a mess, but he seemed sensible enough.

'Yes,' I said. 'I know they're around here. I heard they were at the Red Dragon crater. Do you know where that is?'

'The 20th?' the man asked again. 'They're in 33rd division, aren't they?'

I shook my head, desperately. I didn't know what he meant.

'33rd,' he said. 'Look. You see that man there?'

He nodded through the window. There was enough light sweeping across the platform now to see well enough, but there were a lot of men, and I didn't know who he meant.

'Him, the corporal. The short one. He's in the Royal Welch. They're in the 33rd, too. Ask him.'

I saw who he meant.

The train gave a powerful lurch as the engine was uncoupled and started to move to the other end for the journey back.

I jumped from the train on to the platform, and ran to the corporal from the Royal Welch.

I grabbed him.

'Do you know where the 20th Royal Fusiliers are?'

He turned and his eyes widened when he saw me.

'The 20th. Have you seen them?'

He said nothing, still too surprised to speak. I saw him look over my shoulder, but I kept on, begging him to understand, and finally he did.

'The 20th,' he said. His voice was just like Evans's. 'Yes. They were with us. But the whole division has moved; we were relieved a couple of days ago. I'm the last of the Royal Welch. I got stuck. The rest of the boys have gone, and the 20th would have been with them.'

I felt sick, too sick almost to speak.

'Where?' I said, my voice failing. 'Do you know where they've gone?'

He shook his head, and I thought it meant he didn't know, but that wasn't the reason.

'The Somme,' he said. 'They've all gone to the Somme. It's all quiet here now. That's where they need the men. What's all this about?'

I was in completely the wrong place.

In a daze, I was aware that the corporal glanced over my shoulder again.

'I think someone wants to talk to you.'

I turned and saw in front of me two burly-looking soldiers, wearing the red caps that I knew marked them as military police. A third stood by the steps to the train, talking to the Sister who I'd met on board. She was pointing in my direction.

'I'm not a spy,' I said, but it was no good.

They weren't listening.

211

*T*hey're too busy to know what to do with me. That's what it seems to come down to.

On the face of it I'm just a crazy girl who got herself dressed up as a nurse, but there's always the possibility I'm a German spy. I wouldn't be the first. And if they think that I am and they prove it, then I'll be shot.

I can't speak a word of German, but then, I'd pretend not to, if I were a spy. So I might be a spy or I might just be a nurse who's gone a bit mad, or I might not be a nurse at all. The trouble is they're too busy to find out which. A young woman does not travel around freely in a war. Even nurses are confined to certain times and places; in hospitals, in billets, on trains. I didn't know how to be a nurse in a war well enough, and so I was discovered and traced eventually.

I was brought here, to this army base.

I have no idea where I am. I'm being kept in a tent, which doesn't seem much of a prison, but then I suppose they're not used to having female prisoners. Anyway, there's always a guard on the door, so I can't go anywhere. And even if I could, what would I do?

I was brought here on Monday. I've been interrogated by all sorts of people; there have been cables and 'phone calls, I know, but they still don't know who I am. For the time being I think they've given up.

I've told them my real name, and that I'm not a spy, and that my father is an important doctor and if they shoot me they'll be in awful trouble. But that's all I've said. I hope it's enough.

The worst thing is thinking about Tom.

I have felt nothing of him for days, and I fear that it might be too late.

That it might be over.

I've had the best part of three days to sit and think.

I've been thinking about Tom mostly, but Edgar keeps coming to my mind too. I've had a glimpse of what he went through, and it makes me angry and sad to think of it. What it did to him, how it made him and Tom fight. And all of us. It pulled us all apart.

Still I have felt nothing of Tom. No dreams.

At first I was able to talk to the guard on duty outside the tent. He was obviously mystified about having to guard a young woman, and seemed happy to talk, although nervously at first.

When I told him I wasn't a spy, that was good enough for him, and then he spoke about himself, the war and anything I put into his head.

He patted his leg, which didn't move properly, and said he was glad not to be at the front anymore, but that he hated the job he had now. He said he'd guarded more than one man on court martial offences, and that last week he'd had to watch over a private before he went to the firing squad.

I didn't believe him at first. I couldn't believe we were shooting our own men, but he said the boy had run away from the battle when an attack was on. That was desertion and the punishment was death.

Then someone must have noticed that he was standing inside the door of the tent and not outside, because he was replaced by not one, but two surly soldiers who said nothing to me, no matter how hard I tried to get them to talk.

Since then I've spoken to no one.

22

$\mathcal{B}$efore my friendly guard was replaced, I asked him about the Somme.

He'd heard talk was spreading about some of the engagements, but his knowledge was scant. He'd been in the trenches himself, last summer.

'Where?' I asked him.

'Place called Neuve Chapelle.'

'Was that where you got wounded?' I asked.

He shook his head.

'No,' he said, and laughed a quick, short laugh. 'I was a proper hero in the trenches. Neuve Chapelle turned into a right fiasco, but I was a real hero. I went on five raids. Never got hurt. Not even a scratch.'

He told me about the raids. Four or five men, and an officer, would creep out through our wire at night, armed to the teeth. They might be just having a look at the enemy lines, they might be going to try to kill Germans.

They'd crawl on their bellies over the mud, around the shell-holes, right up to the German wire, sometimes through it, freezing if a flare went up over them, then on again when it went dark.

'The first time I went . . .' he said, and then gave me such a

216

look I knew what he meant. He was scared fit enough to die from it.

'But I went back, and back again, with my stick . . .'

'Stick?'

'Oh, yes,' he said, cheerfully. 'We made a lot of our own weapons. We're supposed to use bayonets in the trenches, but that's no good on a night raid. So we make all these things. Like a policeman's truncheon, say, but with spikes like you don't want to see. Some lads prefer a good big knife. Easier to use when you get into a trench.'

I didn't say anything and he changed the subject.

'But that's not how I got my leg. That was an accident. We was having a demonstration, of a new grenade. Up to then, we'd been making our own bombs. We'd get jam tins, and pack them full of nails and the like, and the charge. The explosive charge, yes? Not very reliable.

'So there was a new bomb they was showing us. A metal canister, packed full of shrapnel. There's this corporal showing us. He's supposed to throw it over a heap of turnips, but his aim is off and it falls short. We all dive to the ground, like crazy, like we're going to get it.

'Then there was a bloody great bang, and a load of turnips flying through the air. Everyone bursts out laughing, and gets up. Then I tries to get up, and found I couldn't. Bit of shrapnel. That was the end of my time at the front.'

He laughed.

Later, I thought about him on his raids, with a weapon in his hand. Presumably he had killed at least one man. Maybe several. He was a friendly man, he seemed very ordinary, kind even, but he didn't seem to be bothered by what he'd done.

And when he got to the German trenches he must have met German soldiers, who would have killed him too, if they could. I wondered if either Englishman or German had the slightest idea what they were killing each other for.

*E*ach night as I lay down to sleep in the tent that has become my prison, I hoped to sense Thomas. He seemed to have gone quiet on me, but at last he is back.

With no one to talk to, no one near, I have had no premonition in days, not even a hint of that itch Jack spoke of. Although I hate it, and dread its coming, when it suddenly vanished, I felt lost without it.

Then, last night, I dreamed.

There was Tom. He had his back to me, he was walking away from me. He was in the countryside somewhere, in a wheatfield on a beautiful rolling hillside. Away on the horizon was a lush green wood, in the full glory of summer, the trees thick with leaves.

I could only watch; I felt like a mere observer, unable to take part in this dream.

Tom held his right arm out to one side, and then I saw the bird perching there. At first I thought it was a bird of prey; he held it as if it were a falcon. But then he gave his arm a gentle lift, and the bird took wing, and then, of course, I saw it was the raven.

It flapped lazily into the air, and wheeled around, coming back towards me in a wide circle, just to let me know that it knew I was there. The raven flew by and I heard it flapping away behind me. Then it must have turned, because it came forward again.

It passed me, then passed Thomas, too, and headed towards the wood. The wheat withered and died where its winged shadow fell. As it flew on up the hillside, the blight spread with it, and the hill became a quagmire of sticky mud, pitted with shell-holes and strewn with wire.

Then the bird reached the lovely wood, which mutated before my eyes into a square mile of splintered trunks and stumps. Those were the strange spikes I'd seen before, and not understood. I knew them now for what they were; a wood that had been murdered. Killed by days of shelling.

It was another nightmare, but my spirits rose nonetheless. I am used to horror now, and the dream told me something I needed to know.

Tom is still alive, because I saw him in my sleep last night. More than that, I sensed him as a living being.

There is still time.

There is still time.

But the reality of my situation is that I am imprisoned.

Trapped. Two guards outside the tent.

I had to do something to get out. I looked at the back of the tent. Only a tent, after all. Very soon they would surely move me to a proper prison somewhere, and then I would truly be stuck. I decided to wait until dusk before trying anything.

The day dragged so very, very slowly, but at last, the light began to fail. Through the tent flaps, I could see that there was now only a single guard outside. They must have decided that two was a bit much to guard one girl.

I watched the guard, what I could see of him, for a long time. He didn't move, at least the back of his right leg and the right side of his back remained motionless, and I watched him for more than half an hour.

As usual, outside, I could hear the noises of the camp. Men calling orders, vehicles rumbling by, shouts, some laughter.

I took another look at the guard, and crept to the back of the tent. I did it slowly. I used my watch, and made myself take ten minutes over it. I lay down on the ground and, taking a deep breath to try to calm myself, I peered under the flap.

All I could see was grass and more canvas. There were other tents nearby. Maybe if I could get out I could lose myself among them.

With a slippery wriggle I forced myself under the tent wall. I was halfway under when I realised that the pegs were too close together. I was stuck. I gave an almighty heave with my shoulders and slid out from the canvas.

'Just how stupid do you think I am?'

I rolled over and looked up into the face of my guard.

I spent the rest of the night lying on the bunk in the tent, staring at the canvas, tears rolling down my cheeks. In the distance I could hear the sound of big guns.

I called Tom's name over and over softly to myself, hoping he could somehow hear me, though I knew he could not.

*N*ow, the tent is far behind me.

Early this morning I was woken by what I thought was a rumble of thunder. Then I heard the murmur of voices outside. I could only catch snippets of the discussion.

'. . . move her . . . Etaples.'

I couldn't hear the reply, just a tone of dissent, but I knew then that my chances of escaping were over.

The discussion outside continued.

'. . . all right. Wait here . . .'

Then silence, followed by the sound of retreating footsteps.

A second later, the flap of the tent was pulled open, and a large soldier came in, ducking under the low doorway.

I stood up to meet my fate, and then, as he raised his head, I saw who it was. My heart leapt.

Jack.

Before I could say anything, he put his finger to his lips, and gave me a look that told me he wasn't meant to be here.

'Do you want to get out of here, or not?' he whispered.

I nodded dumbly.

'Put this around you,' he said.

He swung off his greatcoat and handed it to me.

'We don't have much time. My bike's outside.'

'But how did . . . ?' I stuttered, confused, half asleep.

'Not now!'

It was still early as we put our heads out into the camp. No one was around. Our guard had vanished, though I didn't understand where he'd gone.

And there was Jack's motorbike, its engine the only warm thing in a cold, dew-laden summer morning. Condensation dripped from the tip of the exhaust into the damp grass. Never had a thing looked more beautiful to me. I did the greatcoat up. It swamped me. I pulled the huge collar up and around my hair. I could hardly see, and hoped that that meant no one could see me inside.

'Hold on tight,' Jack said, as we climbed aboard. Once again I rode side-saddle, and we roared away, passing out of the camp so quickly I barely saw the place I had been held captive.

Now we are somewhere in the French countryside. Jack told me the camp was just outside Bethune. We drove as far as a village called Dieval on the main road, then Jack turned off on to roads that are only farm tracks. He said that it was too dangerous to move on the main roads.

I wondered how he knew where he was going at all, but he seemed to know everywhere, without even using a map.

When I asked him about it, he laughed.

'It's my job!'

He's spent months riding all over the same small area of France, here and there and back again, avoiding trouble, learning the best routes. I suddenly felt safe, for the first time in weeks.

18

*W*e headed to the south of Bethune, into the deepest countryside. We found a small stone hay barn at the back of a wood, and rested there.

At last, I had the chance to ask Jack all the questions in my head. He seemed quite amused by it, and I felt he was somehow different from the last time we had met.

As we spoke we sat on a cattle trough under the eaves of the barn. We felt safe; there was no one around. In front of us was a landscape of great beauty. It had been a misty start to the day, a typical summer's morning mist, which had turned into a drizzle of rain.

'Lovely, isn't it?' Jack said. 'Reminds me of home a little.'

'Where's that?' I asked.

'Hereford. I grew up on a farm. It rains there in the summer, too.'

He smiled. As the rain eased off, woodpigeons began to call to each other in the treetops above us, but there was no other sound than the dripping leaves.

'The fields, the woods, the low hills. But just think. If we got on my motorcycle and rode twenty miles that way . . .'

'What?' I said.

'They say it's the closest thing there'll ever be to Hell on earth.'

He paused.

I thought of Tom. Of Edgar.

'What's it like?'

He shook his head. The same shake of the head that the Royal Welch corporal had given me when he said, the Somme.

'We've destroyed it,' he said. 'All this. All that you can see here is gone. There are few trees, no grass, no buildings, no birds. No creatures but the rats and lice.'

He didn't talk about the men who were dying, and something made me not mention it. I didn't know why, but he seemed more upset about the landscape than the men.

'Mud, and wire. Mud and wire, and holes in the ground. If we keep digging long enough maybe we *will* find Hell.'

'But when the war is over, it'll grow back,' I said.

'When the war is over?' he said, shaking his head again. 'You haven't seen it. Nothing could ever grow there again. Nothing.'

We were silent then, and thinking I might have upset him. I changed the subject.

'What were you doing in Bethune?' I asked. 'The chances of you just finding me . . .'

'. . . were nil,' he said. 'That's because it wasn't chance. I came to find you.'

That surprised me for a start, but I should have known. He had planned everything.

'You're big news in Boulogne,' he said, grimly. 'Quite the celebrity. Some say you went mad over your husband. Others have you down as a German spy. I even heard one story that you're a Russian princess, though God knows what they think you would be doing here!'

A Russian princess. With a sick stomach I thought of Mother. Where was her little Sasha now?

'Don't look so worried,' he said. 'You're safe enough. For now. The more nonsense talked about you, the harder it will be for anyone to get to the truth. And only you and I know the truth, don't we?'

I thought of Millie, but I had even lied to her.

'Yes,' I said, 'but I still don't understand . . .'

'. . . how I found you?' he asked, but that wasn't my question. My question was, why?

'When I heard the stories in Boulogne, I knew immediately you'd got yourself into hot water. It wasn't hard to find out where you'd gone, so I got myself a job riding to Bethune. Swapped a run with another rider.

'I watched the camp yesterday, but I wouldn't have known where you were if you hadn't tried your escape by the back-door.'

I felt embarrassed at the thought of it, but Jack shrugged.

'You tried. You're a brave girl, that's for sure.'

'But how did you get the guard to leave?'

'It was easy. He'll be in trouble, but I don't suppose they'll be too bothered finding you. I came up to him, told him I was to move you to a prison camp. He looked doubtful, but I just kept on. It's amazing what people will believe, if you believe it yourself. I suppose he was confused because no one's had to guard a nurse before!

'I brought a sealed envelope. Waved it at him, said it was my orders, but if he wanted to check he'd have to take it to the officer commanding.

'So I gave him the envelope and he went. I offered to guard you while he was gone. He even said thanks!'

Jack smiled and I laughed.

Above our heads there was a rustling in the treetops, but it was just some birds flapping in and out of the shadows. We watched a pale sun peer through the last of the mist in the field in front of us.

I looked down, and saw a raven right in front of us, no more than twenty feet away, hopping across the ground.

It stopped, and cawed.

I screamed, and fell to the ground.

When I woke it was dark. Pitch black. I felt straw under me, and from the way sound died around me I knew I was inside the hay barn.

'Are you awake?'

It was Jack. He was somewhere away in the darkness. I could smell petrol from the bike, the dryness of the hay, and that was about all.

The rest of what happened came back to me. I remembered seeing the raven, and falling to the ground.

I think I was coming in and out of consciousness, sleeping, waking, dreaming, waking again – in such a state of confusion that I had little idea what was real and what was not.

'You've been in a bad way,' Jack said. 'It was the raven, wasn't it?'

'I'm just tired,' I said. 'And hungry too.'

But he was right, it was the raven. A perfectly common bird, but the shock of seeing it had done something to me.

So I spent half the day in a hallucination of fear and dread.

I saw things.

I don't want to think about the things I saw, but when I finally woke up, Jack seemed to know.

'You can feel them, too, can't you?' he said.

'What?' I said, finding my voice. 'Who?'

'The dead,' he said, simply. 'They pull at me when I'm asleep sometimes.'

I nodded, but it was dark, and Jack couldn't see.

'I really am hungry,' I said.

'I know,' he said. 'I went to try and find a farm while you were asleep, but I didn't want to leave you for long . . . Have some water and we'll find food tomorrow.'

He shuffled towards me in the dark and I heard him lighting a match. In the flickering match-light, I saw the barn around us, stacked high with hay, and Jack's face in front of me, grimy, and worn deep with lines. His pale blue eyes seemed lifeless.

'Quick,' he said, holding his water bottle in one hand, the match in the other. 'Before it goes out.'

I took the drink gratefully, but the bottle was nearly empty.

'Tomorrow,' I said.

'What about it?'

'I must find Thomas.'

The match went out and plunged us back into darkness.

'No,' Jack said. His voice was dry, and quiet. I knew he was holding something back.

I didn't answer, hoping he would say more, but he didn't.

'What do you mean?' I asked.

Suddenly I felt scared, sitting alone in the middle of the French night with a man I didn't know. A man who most people considered mad, at that.

'I said, no.'

'But what else are we doing here? Why did you help me get away if not for that?'

He lit another match, studied my face. I glared back at him, my breath coming heavily.

'I got you out because I didn't want anything to happen to you. I want you to go home to England. I want you to be safe.'

'But Tom . . .'

'Is dead already.'

'No!' I cried. 'That's not true.'

'If you've seen him killed then he's as good as dead. There's nothing we can do to change the future. Don't you understand that yet?'

'No!' I shouted. 'He's not dead.'

'Not yet!' Jack shouted back.

He cursed as the match went out.

I began to cry in the darkness.

'You don't understand,' Jack said. 'Why don't you understand? The future's already done! How else do you and I make sense of what we see? What you have seen will come to be and there's nothing you or I can do to change that.'

'I thought you had changed your mind,' I said, through a mouthful of tears. 'What I said that night. That we have to play our part anyway. I thought you understood that. I thought you'd come to help me play my part. I can't simply let him die!'

Jack said nothing, and I listened to myself crying, and hated myself. Edgar was right. I'm just pathetic. Weak.

'Alexandra,' Jack said. 'Don't cry. I'd like to help you. Don't you understand that? I got you out of Bethune because I want to help you. But there's nothing we can do . . .'

'If he was your son, would you let him die?' I sobbed. 'I've already lost one brother. I can't watch it happen again. If I hadn't been given this curse then I wouldn't know any different. Maybe that would be easier. But I can't help it. I have seen Tom and I am going to try to save him. I'd like to say I can do it without you, but I can't. I know that. I need your help.'

Still Jack was silent.

'Why are you helping me?' I asked. 'Why set me free, when you don't want to help me save Tom?'

'I want to help you. I said that.'

'Because I remind you of someone?' I said spitefully, 'Is that it? Your daughter? Your wife?'

'No,' said Jack. 'I'm not married. There's no one like that.'

'Then why?'

'Because, Alexandra, you're the one person I've met in this war whose life I might be able to change.'

'So you *do* think lives can be changed then?' I asked.

Jack was silent.

There was silence for a long time, but in the end I convinced him. I don't really know how. I know Jack is a man who had all belief and hope taken from him long ago. But something I said seemed to make a difference. He lit a third match in the silence, and shuffled over to me. I didn't like him coming that close, but I couldn't say so. I thought it wouldn't be wise to anger him again. He was so near to me that I could smell him, his unwashed skin and clothes. His face was deadly serious.

He looked deep into my eyes, and he was so close I could see the match reflected in his. He put out a shaking hand towards me, and stroked my hair, just once. I closed my eyes and tried not to shudder.

When I opened my eyes again, he was sitting away from me, his eyes closed, his head bowed. He was motionless, as if deep in some dream.

The third match went out.

'I'll help you,' he said.

*J*ack is sleeping, but I slept enough in fits and starts during the afternoon and am not tired.

I do not want to sleep again, in case I see those things, those dead people again. I cannot prevent one thing from surfacing in my mind however. Amidst all the terrible things I saw, I had another sight of Tom.

I saw the gun that will kill Tom, and I flew with the bullet, spinning, spinning towards him. I was so close to it all, I could smell it. I could taste the cordite from the cartridge.

The bullet struck his chest, and I followed only a moment behind.

25

The last two days have been a lifetime.

I think it can barely be thirty-six hours, in fact, since we left the safety of the hay barn, to where I am now.

Where I am now.

From what I can see in the valley below me, this can only be one place.

The mouth of Hell.

*W*e left the barn early.

We were both awake to hear a deafening chorus of birdsong in the wood behind the barn, but though the birds were singing, it was a desolate morning, with a lowering bank of cloud above us. A mild drizzle gave way to maybe an hour of insistent rain, but we left anyway, because we were hungry.

'We'll head for Doullens,' Jack said. 'We can find food there.'

I suddenly worried that maybe Jack was going to change his mind about helping me find Tom, but I needn't have.

'Doullens is quite a big town,' he said. 'There're a couple of railheads there. Supply dumps. And at least two casualty clearing stations, that I know of. There're lots of people. If your brother's division came through, we might find someone who's seen them.'

We rode on the motorcycle across the wet French country-side. It was hard going. The roads we chose were small ones, that had been subjected to less traffic, but nevertheless the thin tyres on the bike cut into the mud at times and we nearly got stuck twice.

By mid-morning we came over the crest of a low hill and saw an ugly little town in front of us. Jack brought the bike to a standstill as the lane we'd been using joined the main road into Doullens.

He seemed to be weighing things up.

'Jack . . .' I said.

He looked at me, and I knew what he was thinking. Even from this distance I could see he was right about the town. It was busy, full of people, soldiers. A hive of comings and goings. I looked down at myself. Still in my uniform, though soaked with rain and mud, with Jack's greatcoat wrapped around me. I would attract attention immediately.

'You're going to have to stay up here,' he said.

'No . . .' I said, but I knew he was right.

'We passed a copse a couple of miles back,' he said. That will have to do.'

It felt awful to have to turn round and retrace our steps even a hundred yards, but I told myself that until we had news of where Tom was, it made no difference which direction we went in.

Jack left me at the copse.

'Stay hidden,' he said. 'I'll be as quick as I can.'

I scrambled into the trees, until I thought I was out of sight, and turned in time to see Jack and his motorbike disappear.

I sat down in the wood, and began shivering almost immediately. The rain had stopped, but I was wet through.

Above me in the sodden treetops, birds jumped and shrieked noisily. I looked up, fearing what I would see. Even the thought of the raven was nearly enough to push me again into a terrible vision of the bird that kept stalking my imagination and my dreams.

I hoped Jack wouldn't be long.

13

*M*aybe a couple of hours later Jack came back. I heard the hum, and then the throb of the motorcycle engine, but I waited until I was sure it was him before walking to the edge of the trees and showing myself. Having sat in the cold for all that time my legs didn't move properly and I feared he might miss me as I staggered out, but he had seen me all right.

'Not a bad place,' he said.

'Any news?' I asked.

He shook his head.

'Sorry. Nothing.'

I felt panic rising, and had to fight to control it.

'It doesn't mean anything,' he said. 'We'll go on to Amiens. It's most likely they were entrained to Amiens, if they're heading up to the Somme. Someone there might have seen them. Be hard to miss a division on the march.'

'Why don't we just go straight to the Somme?' I asked.

Jack laughed, then stopped abruptly when he looked at me.

'If it were that easy . . .' he said. 'We can travel quite fast back here. I know it seems slow, but at the front . . . No one goes anywhere quickly. The roads, if there are any, are thick with mud. And the front is full of people. Don't forget that. The closer we get to the front, the less like this it will be. We haven't passed anyone else all morning, have we? I could just about get away with it, I am a dispatch rider, after all. But you . . .'

I saw what he meant.

'We'd be stopped in no time,' he said.

I nodded.

'So we need to know exactly where he's gone first.'

I thought I might start to cry then, but Jack reassured me.

'Don't worry. We'll find him.'

I wished I shared his belief.

'Breakfast,' said Jack, swinging a bag from his shoulder. 'Or is it lunch?'

'I think it's last night's supper,' I said.

The bag was large, but I was disappointed to find that it was not all food. After pulling out a loaf and some soft cheese, the rest of the bag contained clothes.

A uniform.

'What's that for?' I asked.

'For you,' Jack nodded. 'Put it on. We might pass you off for a soldier from a distance, and besides, they're dry and you're not.'

We ate.

'I thought you told me once that this wasn't a fairy tale. That I couldn't dress myself as a man and get away with it.'

'I said a lot of things,' he said, and turned his back. 'But it can't hurt, anyway. Get changed, then we'll head for Amiens.'

I tiptoed a little way back into the wood, and pulled off my nurse's uniform. As I reached for the clothes Jack had brought me, I saw with revulsion that there were holes and blood-stains in the tunic. I wondered where he had got them, but it was obvious really. He had said there were casualty clearing stations in Doullens. I saw the regimental badge on the shoulder of the tunic, but didn't recognise it. It meant nothing to me.

I pulled the clothes on, waves of different feelings washing over me. I realised how comfortable I felt in my VAD uniform, how I belonged in it. I knew who I was. As I dressed myself in a dead soldier's clothes, it made me feel fragile and weak. I saw my pale girl's skin slip inside the rough cloth of the uniform, and almost laughed at the stupidity of it all. I didn't belong in this world.

The uniform was too big for me, but not by so very much. And then, as I was turning the trousers up, a vision came to me and I knew it was how the man had been wounded. A wound from which he had later died.

I was wrapped in the soldier's dead-world, and could not shed it. I had to wear these clothes if I were going to find Tom. I looked at my nurse's uniform on the wet earth of the copse.

I picked it up and made my way back to Jack.

'What shall I do with these?' I asked.

'Leave them here,' he said. 'Come on. We should go. The heat from the bike will warm you up again, at least.'

Something felt wrong to me. I couldn't just drop my uniform in the mud. I folded it up neatly, and made a small pile, finishing with my apron with the red cross uppermost. I placed it at the foot of a tree just inside the copse, and then turned to Jack.

'Let's go,' I said, and swung my legs over the parcel rack of the bike properly, now that I was wearing trousers.

We left.

I squinted into the wind as we rode.

After a few miles, I imagined the dirty, stolen uniform that had become mine for a short while, lying in a wet French wood.

Then, I suddenly remembered that I had left my Greek book with the uniform. In the rush I'd forgotten all about it. I imagined what someone might think if one day they found a nurse's uniform and a small book of Greek myths in English on the edge of a French wood. Would they ever guess even part of the story behind it?

It was too late to go back for the book, and as we rode I couldn't help but feel I'd lost my lucky talisman.

*B*elow me, as I sit here waiting, I take the occasional peep down into the valley. My eyes grow wide at the sights I see. The men. Thousands of them. The guns. Hundreds upon hundreds of big guns. The horses. The tents, the equipment, the cooking wagons, the ambulances. In a muddy field in the middle of France.

I think back to the last steps of our journey here, through smashed villages and rolling open downs, to this awful, awful place.

'You don't look much like a soldier,' Jack said, as we stopped to rest.

'What do I look like?' I asked.

'Nothing,' he said. 'You're too pretty to be a man, even under all that mud. And too thin. But you couldn't be a girl. Who'd think that? And there are some young boys out here. Very young. The ones that lied about their age so they could come.'

I shrugged.

'You don't look like anything,' Jack repeated. 'Your hair. That's the problem.'

I had tied my hair up, but I knew again he was right. Even

241

though I had clumsily shortened it once before, and even though it was wet and dirty, there was just too much of it.

Jack fished around in the pannier on the bike, and pulled out a knife. A big, sharp knife.

He didn't have to say anything.

And I said nothing in return.

I took off the greatcoat and laid it across the seat of the bike so it wouldn't get any muddier. Then I stood before Jack and bowed my head.

Jack lifted the knife towards me, and took a tress of my hair in the other hand. He cut, and all too easily I watched my hair fall in clumps around my feet. I remembered having my hair cut as a little girl by Mother, and smiled bitterly to myself at these so different circumstances. And if a few tears ended up with my hair in the French mud, no one but me knew it.

'I'm no barber,' Jack said, after a while. It seemed to be taking forever. The big locks had come off easily, but as he got closer to my scalp, it was harder work, and he had to saw the hair off with little jerking motions.

At last it was over. I felt my head, and couldn't believe it was mine. My long flowing hair had been replaced by short, clumsy spikes, an inch or so long, no more.

'It's just as well we have no mirror,' I said.

Jack opened his mouth, then shut it again.

He looked at me sadly.

'Sorry,' he said, 'You're still too beautiful to be a soldier.'

I turned away, embarrassed. I wished he wouldn't say things like that. When I turned back, Jack was pumping the starter pedals of the bike. It roared to life, and he held out the coat for me again.

'Getting low on petrol,' he said. 'We can't afford to mess around.'

Around us the landscape had changed. As we skirted the edge of Doullens we had come into a different type of countryside. The land now was more open, rolling downs criss-crossed with fields, and fewer trees. Bleak. Even the mud clogging our wheels and our boots was different, a sticky grey paste that tugged at us, slowed us down.

Jack had decided that we could risk the main road to Amiens.

'Just keep your head inside that coat if we pass anyone.'

But we saw no one. It was as if the world had ended, and everyone was dead except Jack and me.

On the main road we had made good time to Amiens, but as we neared the city Jack once again steered away from the place itself.

'Where are we going?' I shouted over his shoulder.

He shouted something back, but I couldn't hear what he said over engine noise. It made no difference. I had to trust him, in everything now. I had no other choice.

Finally we began to see people. I clung desperately to his back and hid my face as we passed a column of soldiers marching into the city. Trucks rolled here and there, and I even saw a red cross on one and knew it was a motor ambulance.

The bike stopped.

There was a river in front of us. Not vast, but wide enough and smooth flowing. A stone bridge spanned it.

'That's the Somme,' Jack said. 'Across the other side is a place called Longueau. If they came down from Bethune by train, this is where they'll have come.'

We crossed and came to Longueau, to the station, which was just about all there was of the place.

We parked the motorcycle by the wall of the station. It was late afternoon and although it's July, the sky was heavy and grey and the light was bad.

'Right,' Jack said. 'I'll do the talking. You stay with the bike. If anyone asks, you're a new dispatch rider and I'm teaching you the ropes.'

'Is that going to fool anyone?'

Jack hesitated.

'No,' he admitted, looking at me. 'No. Just pray no one comes near you.'

Jack trotted up the steps into the station. As I waited I tried to look nonchalant, and turned my back on the world if anyone came by, pretending to fiddle with the engine on the bike as I had seen Jack do. I thought it would probably do no harm to get some of the mud off it, and was so busy doing this that I didn't notice Jack had come back.

'Cardonette,' he said, quite quietly, but I could see he was excited underneath. 'They marched from here to Cardonette, Four days ago.'

'Four days?' I cried.

'Not so loud,' Jack hissed. 'They're hundreds of men on foot. We're on a bike. We can catch them up.'

22

Cardonette turned out to be back the way we had come – in fact, we had passed within a mile of it earlier. But we weren't to know that.

It was evening by the time we got there, and with night falling I felt less conspicuous. We risked riding right into the heart of the village, passing by a tented village of soldiers in the fields as we did so. I craned my neck and strained my eyes, trying to see if I could recognise anything that might lead us to Tom, but Jack told me to keep still.

'Have you any idea how many soldiers there are out here? How many units? How many battalions? If we have to find a needle in a haystack, then at least we need a clue where to look.'

So I waited outside while Jack went into an estaminet for more information.

He came back very quickly.

'This is it?' I asked.

'No, but we're getting there,' he said. 'The 33rd was here, and with it, the 19th brigade. Your brother's battalion is in the 19th.'

'But where have they gone?'

'A place called Daours. It's back down on the Somme, near where it meets the Ancre.'

'Can you be sure they were here?'

'Oh yes,' Jack said. 'They remember them well, here. The locals were forced to give their houses as billets for the soldiers. They don't like that. They have every reason to remember them.'

We were getting closer to Tom, but not close enough.

'When were they here?' I asked.

'They left on Tuesday, three days ago.'

'Then we have to hurry,' I said.

'No,' said Jack. 'It's getting late; we're tired. We'll find a bed here and go on in the morning.'

'No!' I said.

'Alexandra . . .'

'No,' I said again. 'We have to go on. I'm not tired. It's not that late. And it's much safer for us to travel in the dark anyway. You know I'm right.'

And for once, Jack had to agree.

So we moved on, to Daours.

10

We rode into the night.

It seemed the whole world had shrunk to just us. The two of us; Jack and me. Or maybe the three of us; Jack, me and the motorbike. Maybe I am tired, maybe I am going a little crazy, I thought, as we trundled on the bike through the darkness. But without the bike I would be as lost as without Jack.

The bike's headlight shone dimly in front of us, and Jack was afraid of that – to show a light in the dark – but there was little we could do. It shone ahead of us, just enough to see the way as mile after mile of narrow, mud-laden track went by under its wheels, while I listened to the sound of the engine rise and fall as it ploughed through the varying ground.

I was sore, sore from holding Jack, my arms felt like lead around his waist. Sore from holding the bike between my legs, sore from sitting on the tiny metal plate.

It was very late by the time we reached Daours, and we repeated the whole performance, while Jack asked around in the village in his excellent French, I lolled on the motorbike, and ignored anyone who came my way.

The news was bad.

'They were here,' Jack said, till Wednesday afternoon. Then they marched on to Buire.'

'How far is that?' I asked.

'About another ten miles,' Jack said.

I got ready to argue with him, but I didn't have to.

'Come on,' he said. 'We'll find him, I know it.'

'You mean, you've seen it?' I asked, but Jack shook his head.

'No,' he said, turning away. 'No. I just think.'

I wanted to lie down and die. Every bit of me was tired, we had finished our food long ago, and I was ready to give up, but I couldn't. Tom was driving me on.

We got back on to the bike again, and slowly crawled out of Daours towards Buire. The night deepened around us, and through it I saw flashes of light ahead of us.

'Lightning?' I shouted to Jack over his shoulder, but he shook his head, and I understood.

Guns. Big guns were firing ahead of us, though not a sound could be heard over the noise of our engine.

We rode on and I gripped Jack grimly, and in the night and the haze in my head, I saw ravens sweeping through the darkness on either side of the bike. I shook my head to clear the vision, but they would not leave, and I do not know if they were real or not. I shut my eyes and tried to think only of Tom, but whenever I managed to bring him to mind, he was replaced by Edgar, laughing at me, waving a fistful of black feathers in my face.

We reached Buire in the dead of night.

Jack cut the engine and we looked at the sorry little village. A church was its most noble feature, otherwise it was a mess of small terraces and the odd grander house.

Finally I was in the thick of people. Despite the late hour, the village was astir with hordes of soldiers, and more amazing to my eye, horses. Lines of cavalry wound their way around either end of the village, the horses plodding slowly and wearily in some places, proud and fine in others. I stared as a line of Indians made their way past us on horseback, their pointed beards and turbaned heads an almost unbelievable sight.

No one took the slightest notice of us. Everyone was busy doing something, going somewhere, or just being too tired to wonder at a dispatch rider and his passenger in the middle of the night.

Once more Jack made some enquiries, and once more the news was tantalising.

'They were here this morning,' he said. 'They left before noon for Meaulte.'

'How far?' was all I could manage to say.

'I've never been there,' Jack said, 'It's about six miles. The road's easy enough to follow, but I've no idea how long it will take.'

I couldn't believe we were so close to Tom – that we had travelled in a day what it had taken him four days to march. I said so to Jack.

'They stopped for a day or two here. Another day and we'd have met them.'

'So . . . ?' I asked.

'So, they'll be in Meaulte now. They'll be there tomorrow. It's six miles. We can take the chance to rest here.'

I began to protest, but Jack stopped me.

'I can't go on. Alexandra. Please trust me. They'll still be in Meaulte tomorrow morning. We can leave at dawn and then we'll find Tom. But we need to get some rest first.'

I was ashamed at myself, but in truth a part of me was happy to agree with Jack, a part of me that was tired beyond belief and exhausted in mind as well as body.

There were large numbers of soldiers in tents in an old orchard on the edge of the village. We kept away from them, but found a small hay loft nearby. There was just enough room for the two of us.

As I went to sleep I heard the sound of guns. The atmosphere seemed to change around us, seemed to tense, as the low boom and rumble of the barrage reached us from the front line.

But Jack noticed none of this, and was already snoring by my side.

9

*W*ith night came the raven dream.

The dream of Tom, the dream of the bullet, and once more I watched paralysed as with infinite slowness, and in precise detail, I saw the gun fire. There was a bright flash, followed by a loud bang. The bullet hurtled towards Tom, ravens' feathers whirling around him, as if caught in a tornado.

The bullet left a curious trail of cordite behind it, a thin smoke that became unnaturally thick, and began to block my vision. I was blinded by it, until just as the bullet hit Tom, I lost sight of him altogether.

When I woke this morning, the world was shrouded in mist.

8

*T*he mist was thick; so thick I could barely see twenty paces ahead.

I woke first, and shook Jack by the shoulder. I have no idea how early it was, but already there were sounds of the encampment stirring and I wanted to be away. I thought of Cassandra, and of the end of her journey. Her story ended in a pool of her own blood on the steps of the palace in Argos. I knew my ending would be very different from hers, and almost as if I had been bereaved, I knew that she was no longer with me.

The mist at least seemed a friend, and hid our progress as we climbed down from the hay loft and wheeled the bike out of the village, without starting it. There was no point in adding to our problems.

We were not alone as we left the village. An almost constant stream of wounded and prisoners approached from the opposite direction, and Jack decided we may as well start the motorcycle again. It looked stranger pushing it than riding it. And the less time anyone had to look at me, the better.

Once or twice I would fancy that someone was looking at me too closely, but no one said anything. Everyone was too busy to worry much about a strange-looking boy on the back of a dispatch rider's motorbike. I suppose the truth is that no one actually looked at me. They just saw another boy in a uniform and left it at that.

We came at last to Meaulte.

The mist was still heavy, but we could see that Meaulte was another drab town. It had a dejected air about it, I thought, as we rode through. A utilitarian, slightly sordid sort of a place, with only its church to be proud of.

And it was there that I thought it was all over.

Jack could find out nothing. Although the place is only a mile or two behind the front, there were still lots of locals in the village. They resented the presence of the war in their world, and the presence of the army.

'Up until a fortnight ago, the front line was just ahead,' Jack said. 'The big push has moved it further east. These people are still scared.'

I couldn't blame them, but I was desperate to find Tom.

'You said they'd be here,' I said angrily, though I knew I'd have been lost without him. I would have got nowhere.

And now, as it is, I seem to have got nowhere anyway.

I am just sitting, waiting, on the edge of death.

*J*ack continued to ask around, and finally found an answer,
but not the one I'd been hoping for.

He came back from a queue of men at a delousing machine
standing at one end of the village. I could tell immediately that
it was bad. He didn't have to say anything.

'They've gone,' I said. 'They've gone, haven't they?'

He nodded, a brief small gesture, but one which dealt me a
massive blow.

'Yes. Before dawn. No one knows where, except that they
were headed for the front. Left most of their kit behind.
They're heading for it, all right. Could be anywhere.'

'But where?' I cried.

'I'm sorry,' Jack said, 'I'm sorry. I don't know. No one seems
to know.'

'What do we do?' I cried. I couldn't admit we were defeated.
It couldn't happen.

'Someone must know something,' was all I could say.

'It's chaos, Alexandra. Nothing's clear. There's fighting
everywhere. There's been a big mauling in a place called
Mametz Wood. I was talking to the lads over there – they're
some of the survivors. We've got control of it now, and the

254

fighting's moved on to some villages beyond. Bazentin, Delville Wood, High Wood. They could be anywhere.'

Something struck me, and I don't know why I bothered to say it, but if I hadn't, then it might all have ended then and there.

'That's strange,' I said. 'Why does it have an English name?'

'What?' Jack said.

'High Wood. Why does it have an English name?'

'That's just what the army calls it. The French call it Raven Wood.'

Raven Wood.

I went cold.

Jack saw; I must have gone as white as death itself.

'What is it?' he said. He grabbed my arm, thinking I was going to faint.

'That's it,' I said. I trembled. 'That's where he's going. High Wood.'

Now I know what the raven means, now at last I can answer that question from my dreams.

I know what the raven means. It means death.

It means High Wood.

It's where Tom is going to die.

I am waiting now, on the edge of a place called Death Valley. That's not its real name, just one given to it by the soldiers. Some of them call it Happy Valley instead, which is supposed to be a joke, but how anyone can laugh here, I do not know. But they do. I've seen them.

Jack knew I was right. He trusts my vision as I believe in his.

As soon as I saw the connection with the raven, it was obvious, and so we made our way here. I was feeling utterly desolate. We were surrounded by men on all sides, streams of troops marching to the front, or staggering back in ragged lines. Once Tom's battalion has gone up to the front itself, I will be unable to reach him. My only hope is that I can get him away before that happens.

We left Meaulte and rode on clogging mud-tracks through the remains of other villages, one of which had only its church tower left standing. I don't know what they were all called, but a place called Fricourt was no more than a vast pile of rubble, with buildings that looked as if they had just collapsed and died.

Further on, small copses of trees lay around us, some intact, some just fields of broken stumps. Jack explained that the front line ran through the area until the big push began a fortnight ago. There's been lots of fighting here, and I cannot describe the things I have seen that prove that fact.

Dead men lie at the side of the road.

Jack rode on, and though I stared, they were soon behind us.

Suddenly, there was a strange whistling hum in the air, and seconds later we were at the edge of a storm. It was not a storm of nature, but one of machinery and artillery.

Explosions ripped the ground ahead of us, and Jack frantically pulled off the road.

'Five-nines!' he shouted. 'Get in that ditch and keep your head down.'

He didn't have to tell me. We flung ourselves from the bike and cowered on the ground until the barrage stopped.

It didn't last long.

'Are you all right?' Jack asked me, as he got to his feet.

I couldn't answer, I was too stunned to speak.

I nodded, mute. We moved on.

Then the bike gave out.

We had been struggling through oceans of mud. The chalky land around us is covered by a thick clay, which had been churned into a grey-brown paste that binds and sticks.

The faithful Triumph had worked its way deep into this mud at the bottom of a hollow, and no matter how much Jack tried we could not shift it.

We got off, and tried to push it free, Jack revving it all the while, but I only managed to lose my footing and fall face down in the mud.

Some Scots were passing. They laughed at me, but I didn't care. No one could recognise me now, I thought, and two of them came over and lifted the bike free with Jack's help, but we had only made our way a little further when it ran out of petrol.

I was too tired even to cry now, and we stood, staring at the useless bike, lying on its side like a dead animal in the mud.

With a strangely unnatural speed, the mist began to clear, the sun burning it off in a matter of minutes, and we could see it was going to be a hot day after all.

We saw we were surrounded by the dead. Bodies lay here and there, uncared for, unburied, almost unnoticed. I tried not to look at them, but couldn't help staring at the huge corpses of horses that lay among the human dead.

The old front line was ground covered with debris, with old and new shell-holes, rifles, clothing, and all sorts of other equipment strewn around and abandoned. I found it hard to take it in. Even the word 'desolation' comes nowhere near describing what I saw. It was a twisted and broken world, made by men.

More wounded came by. Going forwards, streams of soldiers were marching, and more Indian cavalry trotted past on horse-back.

Then, standing, staring in despair at the bike, I looked up at the file of men passing us, and I saw Tom.

Jack saw me start, and before I could call out, clapped a hand over my mouth.

The movement was enough to catch Tom's eye.

I barely recognised him, and as he stared back at me, as he stared straight through me, I realised that he didn't recognise me at all.

Jack stepped back.

'Tom,' I said, mouthing the word at him.

Then he knew me, and a look of terror and wonder spread

across his face. I saw what he saw. A thin, gangly boy, covered in mud, with rough shorn hair. And who looked a little bit like his sister.

He came over to us, glancing nervously back at the line of men he should have been marching with, and at Jack, and at me.

As he came closer I could see he finally believed it was me.

'What?'

That was all he said, and I could not speak.

'Why?' he said. 'Why are you here?'

He glanced again at his battalion, but no one seemed to be bothered that he had fallen out. In fact, it seemed they had reached their destination, for just ahead in a low curve of land, we could see the start of a huge encampment of men, guns, equipment, and horses. Battalions of men were camped around on all sides.

'Why, Sasha? How did you get here?'

He glanced at Jack, then back to me.

'I've come to take you back,' I said at last.

'You've . . . what?' Tom said, perplexed, his face dark.

'I've seen what's going to happen to you,' I said. 'Tom, you must believe me, I've seen what's going to happen. You're going to be killed if you don't come away. You're going to High Wood, aren't you?'

'How do you know that?' he asked, scowling.

'Tom, you have to believe me! You have to, no one else does, but it's true. You're going to be killed.'

'Oh God,' he said. 'Why can't you understand . . . ?'

He reached out to me.

'Go away, Sasha,' he said. 'Go home. Get this stupid man who's brought you here to take you home again. I don't believe

259

you. I don't believe you because it's not true, and even if I did, I wouldn't leave. I can't. I belong with these men. I can't run away because my sister tells me to, and if I did, I'd be shot anyway!'

He stopped, then he turned and looked at his battalion, who were nearly out of sight at the head of the valley.

'I must go,' he said, sadly. 'Go home and be safe.'

He went.

Jack and I argued over what to do, but in the end it was obvious. We had to go home. Tom wasn't going to come, and even if he did, he'd be shot for desertion.

All my hopes and plans lay in ruins. Everything I'd worked for. But I couldn't leave it like that.

I had to talk to him once more, and say goodbye properly. Then I would leave it alone like everyone wanted me to. I knew I couldn't risk being seen in the valley in daylight, and now that the mist had lifted, it was much too risky. We found an out-of-the-way crook at the top of the valley, a little hollow amongst some sickly-looking trees. Away in front of us was the valley, and beyond that, the awful sight of Mametz Wood. The whole place like a biblical scene of pestilence and death.

I begged Jack to go into Death Valley, find Tom and bring him to talk to me.

He agreed, grudgingly, but he agreed.

And that is where I am now, waiting for Tom, to say good-bye.

As Jack left, he lifted his tunic and pulled his revolver out from the case at his hip.

'Here,' he said. 'In case you get into trouble. Just squeeze the trigger. Don't pull. And keep your arm strong.'

He really meant me to use it.

I knew what he was afraid of. If someone came across me, out here, away from the sight of the rest of the men, anything could happen.

I sat down in the hollow, using the greatcoat as a blanket, and waited.

And I am waiting still, for Jack to return with Tom.

If he doesn't, then what?

What if something happens to him? How will I get away then? I will be lost without him, and anything could happen to me. And if it does, my story will stop here, with me in this hole, clutching the revolver tighter with every hour that passes.

My story could end, right here.

5

3

I am blind.
I am as blind as a book with no writing on the page.

2

*B*lind
Slowly, everything came back to me.

But it was a slow and painful recovery, a memory that did not want to come to mind easily, and did so like a difficult birth.

It has all been a bitter joke.

The hours passed, dragged by. Finally, I could stand the waiting no longer, and crept to the top of my little hollow in the trees, and peered down on Death Valley. I can only guess at how many thousands of men were massing there.

It was a vast waiting room, the point at which men and horses and guns were all being gathered in readiness for some terrible battle at the front. I watched streams of horsemen below me, the Indian cavalry again. I almost smiled to see them. Teams of guns were ridden up as well, and thousands upon thousands of men, all milling about in the open, as if it was an expedition and not a war.

I strained my eyes, desperate to glimpse Tom, or Jack.

More than once I thought about going down myself, but I forced myself back into my hollow and lay looking at the sky. I was starving, but what did that matter? There were more important things afoot than hunger.

265

I thought about Jack more than Tom for some reason. I understood that deserters were shot, and I worried that I had got Jack into danger. What if he were accused of desertion? He had been missing for two days now.

I couldn't bear the thought that I might be responsible for getting him shot, because I had only been thinking about Tom.

And Tom. I now realised at last the misconception I had been living under. I'd wanted to mend everything by saving him, to make my family whole again, as whole as it could be, at least, but everything was in tatters.

I couldn't take Tom away, or he'd be shot for desertion too. I knew the only way men got away from the front was with a decent wound.

I clutched the revolver so tightly my fingers ached.

Then, without warning, there was a scrape behind me, and two men came over the lip of the hollow.

It was Tom, and behind him, Jack.

I dropped the gun on the coat and jumped up to meet him, and put my arms around him.

We stayed that way for ages.

I cried, and so did he.

Jack stepped back, then sat down on the ground.

'You haven't got long,' was all he said. He seemed nervous, agitated.

I looked at Tom, and at last I was pleased to see he seemed happy to see me.

'I can't believe you got here,' he said, smiling.

'I've been nursing. In France,' I said. 'But I was just trying to get to you.'

266

'You're amazing,' he said. 'It's hard to . . . but you're here, so it must be true.'

'How are you?' I asked.

Tom shook his head.

'All right,' he said, 'I'm all right. Just tell Mother and Father that.'

I must have looked strangely at him.

'What is it?' he asked. 'Are they all right?'

'I think so,' I said. 'I don't know. Tom, I ran away. They don't know where I am. I did this for all of us, but if I ever get home they'll probably never speak to me again.'

'Of course they will,' Tom said, 'And you must go home. It's wonderful to see you, Sasha, but you must get away from here. It's dangerous, for so many reasons. I spoke to your friend Jack. He's told me what you've done. He says he'll help you get home.'

'Yes, Tom, but . . .'

'No, Sasha, No. I only came up here because Jack assured me you'd seen sense now.'

'You don't know what I've seen,' I said, angrily.

'Alexandra, listen, you have to drop all this talk about seeing the future . . .'

'Why?' I cried. 'Why don't you believe me? Mother and Father wouldn't believe me. Edgar wouldn't believe me. I thought you would, Tom. I need you to. You have to.'

'It's not that easy to understand.'

'Everyone thinks I'm a fool. Edgar died still thinking that. I can't take it from you, too.'

'Edgar didn't think that, I swear,' Tom said. 'None of us do.'

'How do you know what Edgar thought?' I said, bitterly. 'The last time we saw him he was miserable and silent. You weren't even there. Then he went back to the war and was killed.'

'No, Sasha, I did see him.'

I looked sharply at Tom, incredulous.

'He came to see me in Manchester. He said he'd left Brighton a day early to come to see me. We talked like we'd never talked before. It made everything seem right again between us. I felt I understood him, and what he wanted to do. With the war. But he said it had changed him. It wasn't what he was expecting. He said it terrified him. He told me to go on trying to be a doctor. That there was more use in that than fighting.'

I shook my head, struggling to understand what Tom was saying.

'And he talked about you, so much. I know he was difficult with you, but he was proud of you, too. He loved you, Sasha. He really did.'

I said nothing, just stared at Tom.

'It's the truth. Then he went back to the war and he was killed, as you say. When I heard, I wanted to die too, and I couldn't think of any easier way to do it, than to come out here. Do you understand? And I'm going to stay here until either I'm dead, or the war is over.'

I felt utterly empty. I thought back to when Tom had changed his mind about the war, after Edgar died. Edgar had told him to go on with his training, but what had Tom said that day in the kitchen? Mother had begged him to go on being a doctor, and what had he said?

There's no use in it.

So he'd come to fight or die, instead. I would lose both brothers. I saw that now.

268

Tom turned to go. He hesitated, then came towards me, and put his arms around me. As he was breaking away he suddenly froze as he looked at my eyes. He saw something.

'God, no . . .'

Then he shook his head, pulling away, shaking his head as if to clear his vision.

'I'm so tired, I can't . . . I have to go, now, Sasha, you understand that, don't you?'

And I had.

I had understood that he had to go, I really did. I knew there was nothing I could do, that he couldn't walk away from it all.

Unless he was wounded.

I think it was the weeks and days and hours of seeing and hurting and fearing and believing in Tom's death.

That was what made me walk to the greatcoat, and pick up the revolver.

It happened as slowly as it had in my dreams. But this time I saw everything.

I saw Jack's head turn, to see what I was doing. He began to stand, but I had already picked up the gun and pointed it at Tom.

Jack called out.

'No!'

Tom turned.

I pulled the trigger. The gun seemed to explode in my hand, and I felt a kick to my arm. I had tried to aim at Tom's legs, so I wouldn't hurt him too badly, but the force of the recoil sent the gun flying up.

A moment later, Tom lay bleeding on the ground, the trees above him still shaking from the gunshot.

'Oh, Sasha,' Tom said. 'What have you done?'

Blood began to pour from between his fingers as he held them to his chest.

Time stood still.

l

(S)o weeks have passed, and that moment is behind me now, but it leaves behind an awful fact, that it was I who shot Tom.

First, it is true that without Jack, Tom would have died.

As we stood in the hollow, and the harsh reality of what I'd done broke through, I began to shake with fear. Those final moments are unbearable to think of.

Almost as soon as I shot Tom, a flight of shells began to twitter overhead. They landed nearby, with a soft plop into the ground, and no loud explosion.

I didn't understand, but Jack did.

'Gas,' he said. 'Oh God.'

Tom was barely conscious.

But somehow, we got him down from the hollow, and that's when I took the gas. I was lagging behind as Jack carried Tom towards the camp.

Suddenly gas was in my eyes, and my lungs, and though I was sure I was full of it, I must only have had a taste. Nonetheless I was struggling to breath properly. I staggered and fell well behind Jack. Another shell burst somewhere near me, not gas but explosive this time, and that's when I went stopped seeing.

Amidst the chaos from the gas attack, Jack found some stretcher bearers and got Tom to the field dressing station. I stumbled along by myself, then felt Jack's hand. He had come back for me.

I heard voices.

'Poor lad, got a whiff,' someone said.

'We'll sort him out.'

It took me a while to understand they were talking about me. I must have looked so awful they really did think I was a boy. Jack told me later that I was a complete mess. My eyes were watering, my skin was grey. I was covered in mud from head to toe and coughing up great chunks of mucus and fluid from my lungs.

No wonder they didn't see the girl underneath it all.

We got away.

I didn't see Tom again. Jack says he was packed straight off to the ambulance train, and given his Blighty ticket with a good chance of making it. He had a nice clean bullet wound, not some terrible jagged mess from a piece of shrapnel.

I really believe he'll be all right. The visions have stopped.

In fact, for a long time, I had no vision of any kind.

Now, I can see again, but like any normal person, nothing more.

I was put on an ambulance train later, still unable to see, still fighting to breathe, and ended up in Rouen.

And there, as some friendly nurse cut away my uniform, they finally found out I was a girl.

Blind, I reached up and grabbed the nurse's arm.

'Whoever you are,' I said. 'Please help me. I'm a nurse. I swear, I'm a nurse.'

And bless them, they did.

I was put in a private room, and they nursed me back to health, and slowly, ever so slowly, my sight came back.

They said it was a miracle, but I knew I had to see again, and I did.

One day, I had a visitor.

I was sitting in the hospital gardens. It was a warm, hot day at the end of August, and I looked up to see a soldier walking towards me.

It took me a moment to realise it was Jack.

He was different. He was smarter. Cleaner. I had never seen him clean-shaven before, and his hair was smart, too.

'Alexandra,' he said and put his arms around me.

I held him away from me and smiled.

'You can see again?'

'I knew I had to see you again,' I said, and he laughed.

'Your hair's growing back,' he said, as if it were the most amazing thing in the world.

'I've got something for you,' he went on, and pulled a small package from his pocket. 'I went back for it.'

He handed me something wrapped in newspaper, and nodded at me. I opened it. It was Miss Garrett's book of *Greek Myths*.

I began to laugh, with tears in my eyes.

'Thank you, Jack,' I smiled. 'Thank you. I said I'd take good care of it. Now I can send it back to her.'

'It's a little worse for wear,' he said. 'A month in the rain.'

I laughed again and then he told me everything that had happened since the day we'd found Tom.

He'd got away with being absent from duty, he said, by claiming his bike had broken down in the middle of nowhere. He said they just about believed it because it was easier than trying to prove he'd deserted. And after all, he'd come back, and so hadn't deserted in the end, anyway. As for stealing me from the camp at Bethune, there was no proof that it had been Jack who had done it. They seemed to have let it drop.

'There's a war on,' Jack said, grinning. 'Much worse things to worry about.'

We talked for hours in the sunshine.

It was wonderful to see him again, and he told me how much I'd helped him. He said he'd come to a new kind of understanding about his premonitions. That maybe what you thought you saw was not the *only* future, but just *one* possible future. Maybe you could change things to another, different truth if you tried hard enough.

Like I had, he said.

He said he still had visions, but they worried him less, now.

'What about you?' he asked.

I told him that they had gone. That they had left me when I went blind, and so far had not returned.

But still an awful thought hung over me.

I had seen the very thing that had taken me all the way to find Tom, and it was I who had shot him. Maybe none of this had to happen at all, had I not made it.

'Perhaps,' said Jack. 'But your brother would probably have got it, anyway.'

'What do you mean?' I asked.

'His battalion went up from Death Valley to High Wood a

274

few days after we were there. It was a mess. They were annihilated. Almost none of them came back.'

I thought for a while. I realised that I'd never really seen anything about myself. Of course, I'd had the raven dream many times, but never seen that I was the one pulling the trigger.

And somehow, I understood something else. Maybe it had to happen like this. Extraordinary as it is, I think this might be the thing that brings my family back together, in the end. Edgar is gone, but my memory of him is a happy and proud one now, and I know he felt the same about me.

Then something else came to me. I suspected something.

'Why did you agree to help me, Jack?' I asked. 'After you got me out of Bethune, you just wanted me to go home. Did you see what was going to happen? When you touched me?'

Jack sighed.

'Yes. In a way. I couldn't believe it, but I went along with it. I wondered if there was a way out of it for you, after all. I didn't say anything to you. What could I have said? But when I saw you aiming the gun . . . Then I wanted to stop you, but it was too late.'

After a while, Jack left me to my thoughts.

Before he went, we held each other once more.

'Do you see anything?' he asked, looking into my eyes.

'No,' I said. Then, almost too nervous to ask, 'Do you?'

'No,' he said, smiling. 'Just a long and good life. Be happy, Alexandra. You deserve it.'

I waved to him from my bench in the garden as he turned the corner of the hospital, and vanished from sight.

And so I am left alone, but not alone.

I have decided to stay here.

I spoke to the commandant of the hospital here in Rouen, and told her some of my story, though not all of it. I told her I was a VAD nurse who had got into the danger zone, and that all I wanted to do was try to help men get well.

She asked no more questions. They need every pair of hands they can get out here.

One day, I might go home to my parents. I will write to them soon. I don't know what they will say, but for now, I am happy.

It's funny, but out here I often think of Clare. I'm not sure why, but maybe it's because I hope I'm making up for things at last, by helping with the wounded men.

Father didn't want me to be a nurse at all, and now here I am, in a war in France, doing just that. Maybe, like Edgar, he thought I wasn't up to it. But I realised a few days ago that I am. I went all the way to the front to find Tom, and though I was very scared, I did it.

I did it, after all.

So I am happy. I am busy.

The bells are sounding.

Wounded men are coming.

And I must go, I have my work to do.

Author's Note

This is a work of fiction. In order to give it credibility much of it is based on real places and events, but all characters in the story, both in Brighton and the Dyke Road Hospital, and in France, are fictitious. However, instances of reported pre-monition were not uncommon in the trenches, and the epithet 'Hoodoo' is from a genuine case.

The French name for High Wood is not Raven Wood, though this is what Robert Graves asserts in his autobiography, *Goodbye to All That*. It was here that I took the idea for Alexandra's visions, but I have not been able to find any other original source call the wood by that name. The French for raven is *corbeau*, or in the dialect of Picardy, *cornaille*, but the French name was *Bois des Foureaux*, or sometimes *Bois des Fourcaux*. (These names have no obvious translation, the former meaning maybe 'waters of the kiln', but though the wood may have once been the home to charcoal burners, there is no river or stream running through it. I think the name is more likely to be a corruption of *fourchette* – the sweet chestnut trees were used by the local people to make pitchforks.)

Whatever the name of the place, it was here that the 19th Brigade, with the 20th Royal Fusiliers among them, were heading in mid July 1916. On Saturday the fifteenth, they became part of the vast number massing in Death Valley, in readiness for their part in the assault on High Wood. Gas shells fell among them that morning.

On 20 July, their turn came to go up to the engagement in High Wood, and the battalion was almost annihilated.

The official divisional record simply states: *attack continued, extremely difficult to form precis of fighting.*

Marcus Sedgwick
West Sussex
December 2004